A CASE of STRANGULATION
by A Stranger

Texas General Cozy Cases
Of Mystery
Book 3

BECKI WILLIS

Cover Design by Anelia Savova (annrsdesign.com)

Editing by SJS Editorial

ISBN: 978-0-9987902-7-5

OTHER BOOKS BY BECKI

Forgotten Boxes
Plain Roots
Tangible Spirits
He Kills Me, He Kills Me Not
Mirrors Don't Lie Series
The Sisters, Texas Mystery Series
Spirits of Texas Cozy Mystery Series

TABLE OF CONTENTS

CHAPTER ONE 1

CHAPTER TWO 12

CHAPTER THREE 25

CHAPTER FOUR 42

CHAPTER FIVE 53

CHAPTER SIX 70

CHAPTER SEVEN 84

CHAPTER EIGHT 94

CHAPTER NINE 108

CHAPTER TEN 120

CHAPTER ELEVEN 134

CHAPTER TWELVE 143

CHAPTER THIRTEEN 158

CHAPTER FOURTEEN 173

CHAPTER FIFTEEN 188

ABOUT THE AUTHOR 203

CHAPTER ONE

Head Nurse Laurel Benson skimmed the roster for tonight's shift at *Texas General Hospital*. With a big concert in town and an Aggie baseball game at home, the twin cities of Bryan-College Station were buzzing with action. The emergency department was created for nights like this.

Good, Laurel nodded with approval. A solid crew for what promises to be a busy evening. We already have a smorgasbord of ailments. What else will the night hold?

A child with a broken arm occupied Room 1.

An elderly man with a known heart condition was in Room 2, complaining of chest pains and difficulty breathing.

Rooms 3 and 8 had occupants from the same minor fender bender.

Before the concert was halfway through the opening act, an overzealous fan had jumped the barrier, made a mad dash for the stage, and landed herself in Room 4 with a badly twisted knee. If she managed to avoid surgery, Laurel imagined the woman's next dash would be from a jail cell.

Room 5 was being disinfected and deeply cleansed after a patient with a nasty stomach bug.

A rasping asthma patient rested uneasily in Room 6, and, thanks to a wayward fly ball at Olsen Field, a possible concussion sat in 7.

An ambulance was on its way with an occupant for another of the rooms, and the waiting room was already half-full of people biding their time to see a doctor.

They say variety is the spice of life. Only mildly spicy so far, but the night's still young.

Hearing the rattle of a gurney, she glanced up and saw a patient tech easily maneuver an empty bed down the hallway with one hand. "Hey, Laurel. How's it going?" the giant of a man asked.

"Fine, Boomer. Did you get our patient admitted and delivered upstairs?"

"Sure did." He smiled. He slung a lock of sandy-brown hair from his eyes and asserted, "I'll have Room 10 ready to go in two shakes of a frog's hind leg."

Boomer Scott kept the emergency department entertained with his off-the-wall sayings and upbeat sense of humor. In a setting that often saw patients in their worst moments or loved ones confronted with their deepest fears, the cruelties of life could be highlighted in sharp detail. Sometimes, a sense of humor was all that kept the medical team sane. Laurel enjoyed working with the jovial technician, even if she suspected he had an unrequited crush on her.

"Thanks," she told him. "I'm sure we'll need it."

"How's Fly Ball Freddy?" he inquired. The six-foot, two-inch comedian was always the first to assign nicknames for their patients.

"I'm sure he'll have more than a ball as a souvenir of this game. He already has a nice goose egg on his forehead, and there's a black eye in his very near future."

Boomer slowed as he wheeled past the nurses' station. "Ever been to an Aggie baseball game?"

"It's been awhile," Laurel admitted. She had grown up here, but college and a career in one of Houston's busiest hospitals had kept her away for the better part of a decade. In the three years since returning home, she had been too busy settling into a new job and a new house to attend a game.

"If it weren't so dangerous, I might take you to one," he quipped. His voice was playful, but she detected a nervous sheen within his green gaze.

Laurel pretended to shiver. "Not sure I could handle the tension," she claimed.

Sirens wailed, and the doors from the ambulance bay flew open, signaling the arrival of a new patient. Without further flirtation, Boomer pushed off and headed for Room 10. Laurel was hardly surprised by his immediate transformation. In the right setting, Laurel imagined he could be the life of the party; in an emergency setting, he was nothing if not professional. She appreciated his dedication and felt fortunate he was on duty this night.

The call light for Room 6 lit up. "Trevor," she instructed the nurse sitting at the next computer, "you take the ambulance. I'll take 6."

"Yes, ma'am," he said, promptly getting to his feet.

Laurel waited for the scornful look he often tossed her way, pleased when he hurried to the arriving ambulance without a fuss. He was new to the department and still adjusting to the way they did things here at *Texas General*. She suspected he was also adjusting to having someone younger than him in charge. She had yet to celebrate her thirtieth birthday, and he was at least ten years older. For whatever reason, Trevor Winslow appeared to be one of those people who had a problem with the age-to-authority ratio.

Padding down to Room 6, Laurel knocked before pushing aside the curtain. She assessed her patient silently for a moment.

Color is improved. Lips no longer blue, circles under eyes less pronounced. Cheeks and eyes don't appear as sunken. Breathing not as labored; chest moving more freely. No retractions with respirations. Seems to be rebounding from episode.

Infusing her voice with a smile, Laurel stepped further into the room. "Hello, Professor Tonchev. How can I help you?"

The petite woman on the bed offered an apologetic smile. "I'm sorry to be of bother," she said. "I'm rather chilly now."

Laurel's nod was sympathetic. "I know when you're having difficulty breathing, you need as much air as possible. The problem is, once the trauma passes, you become cold. I'll be happy to get you a warm blanket."

"That would be divine," the woman said in her lightly accented voice.

"You seem to be better now?" Laurel made it a question.

"Most definitely." Ylenia Tonchev nodded her dark head. "A fact my students may not appreciate come Monday morning, but I believe I am fit enough to return to class."

"I'll let you in on a little secret." Laurel leaned inward as if to confide a well-kept truth. "We aren't nearly so concerned about those college students as we are about their professor. That was a severe attack you had. You may want to take a few days to recover."

"I will have the weekend," the woman assured her.

"I'm sure Dr. Ainsley will stress this before releasing you but be certain to get plenty of rest and stay hydrated. Avoid any food that has a tendency to trigger your asthma."

"When I was growing up in Bulgaria, my mother made for me a special tea. I keep it on hand for such occasions."

"That's good. Enjoy your special tea while resting in bed," Laurel suggested. "I'll get that heated blanket for you. I'll just be a jiffy," she promised.

Or two shakes of a frog's hind legs. She giggled to herself as she borrowed Boomer's words and pushed aside the curtain, intent on the warming cabinet and its trove of deliciously warm blankets.

A burst of noise and a distressed cry pulled her intent elsewhere.

"Nurse! Help me!"

Laurel jerked around, looking for the voice. To her left, a flurry of activity advanced from the adjacent hallway. Personnel crowded around the incoming stretcher, hooking up monitors and shouting orders as they approached. Boomer came around the corner in a run, pushing a crash cart ahead of him. She saw Dr. Luna grab it from the other end and pull it into the room.

The voice must have come from her right. Laurel swiveled in that direction. A patient from the fender bender had walked to the bathroom unassisted but was now having trouble staying in an upright position. As Laurel rushed over to the man, she read the delayed signs of concussion.

Dizzy. Eyes aren't focused, so most likely blurred vision. Looks a bit nauseous. Pale and sweaty.

As she helped the man steady himself and walk slowly back to his room, she glanced at the crisis still underway at the corner. Once the concussed patient was back in his bed, and Laurel had noted the recently exhibited symptoms in his chart, she ducked out to retrieve the warmed blanket.

She nodded to Boomer as they passed in the hall, his expression grim on his way to another crisis.

Nurse Winslow brushed past her, hurrying toward the activity buzzing at the end of the hall.

Hadn't he been there all along? Laurel was surprised to see him but assumed he had gone after something. It wasn't unusual for someone to dash out of the room, snag a needed item, and be back before anyone noticed they were gone, certainly before a request could go through the front desk, be translated to anyone with a free hand, and delivered to the needed location.

Rather belatedly, Laurel paused outside Professor Tonchev's room to announce her arrival. "Sorry for the delay," she said as she pushed through the curtain, "but I come bearing gifts. One deliciously warm blanket, as promised."

The professor made no comment. Her head lolled to one side as she slept.

Laurel's voice dropped to a soft murmur. "I'll just tuck this around you and let you get some rest." She draped the blanket over the sleeping woman's legs and moved upward, over her waist, and toward her shoulders.

A frown puckered the nurse's brow. Ylenia's chest was eerily still. Worried her asthma had kicked back in, Laurel made certain the oximeter was securely in place as she darted her eyes toward the monitor.

It made no sense. No numbers showed. No alarms sounded.

"What in the..."

Somehow, the monitor had been disengaged.

Laurel jabbed a few buttons, bringing the system back to life. Immediately, alarms beeped, and lights flashed in warning. She jabbed at the buttons again, thinking something was wrong with the monitor. Where were all the numbers?

The screen was blank, but for the solid line. Where there should be rises and dips, dots and dashes, there was nothing but a flat, solid line blinking across the screen. No heartbeat displayed. No oxygen levels.

It can't be!

Laurel jerked back toward her patient. The professor still looked peaceful, her face lax in what Laurel had mistaken for slumber, but she noted the unnatural pallor of her skin.

A sinking sensation rattled the otherwise calm nurse. Sensing the dreaded outcome before she even touched her, Laurel pressed her fingers against the woman's still-warm neck.

No pulse tapped against her fingers.

Ylenia Tonchev was dead.

Laurel and her co-workers tried reviving the professor, working the code until the outcome was inevitable.

Laurel stood back as the doctor called the time of death.

Silence descended upon a room that, only moments before, had been bustling with activity. The staff and attendants bowed their heads in a moment of respect.

It never escaped Laurel's notice that, when moments like these were over, the group quickly dispersed and went back to business. As difficult as it was to lose a patient, there were always others waiting. As health care professionals, they had to ignore their own feelings of sorrow and loss and concentrate on the living. Tonight was no exception.

Yet Laurel lingered in the doorway, the finality of death heavy upon her tender heart.

Boomer came up behind her and gently squeezed her right shoulder. "That was a tough one," he murmured, brushing his hand along her left elbow.

She appreciated the sentiment, but the truth was, they were all tough. She said as much in a broken whisper.

"I just don't understand," she murmured, not for the first time.

She felt Boomer shrug his mighty shoulders and move away. Danni Barrington, another nurse and one of her closest friends, moved into his place.

"I know, sweetie," she commiserated. "It's hard."

"Truly, I don't understand. One minute, she was fine. Improving. Looking forward to her special tea and her classes on Monday. And the next thing I know..." Her voice trailed off as she shook her head with an anguished sigh. "It doesn't make sense."

"Laurel, you can't possibly blame yourself for this."

"I should have noticed something. Surely, there was something I missed. Some symptom I overlooked."

"You didn't overlook a thing. Her vitals were normal. Her breathing had stabilized. There was nothing to indicate she would have a setback and stop breathing, only moments later." Danni expressed her condolences with a gentle back rub.

"Then we've missed something."

"I know it's hard to accept, but we aren't God. We can't always save them."

Laurel's voice was flat with conviction. "But I should have."

Having unhooked and stashed away all monitors and equipment, the last attendant left the room. The professor's body would remain until her family arrived to say their final goodbyes.

Laurel moved forward, searching for any sign she might have missed. The woman's olive skin appeared gray in death, with traces of blue beginning to take over where blood had pooled but no longer flowed. Without the equipment and the frantic efforts of the code team to bring the patient back to life, Laurel had a better view of the professor's neck. She was surprised to see faint streaks of blue encircling the slender column.

"Danni? Take a look at this." Laurel pointed to the place in question. "Do you see what I see?"

Her russet-haired friend leaned closer. "Are those... bruises?" She looked up, a question in her eyes. "Th—Those look like..."

"Exactly!" Laurel's animated response set her dark curls bouncing. "Those look like finger marks. She didn't die from asthma. Someone strangled Professor Tonchev!"

CHAPTER TWO

Laurel requested Dr. Ainsley return to the room, STAT. After careful scrutiny, the physician agreed with Laurel and Danni.

"We'll need to call the police," she said, her voice low and filled with concern. As the attending physician and one of *Texas General's* most esteemed doctors, the sixty-something woman had an air of authority about her. "This room will be strictly off limits. To everyone."

"We could have the night watchman stationed at the door," Danni suggested.

"Good idea," Monica Ainsley said. "Laurel, you were the first to discover her. You'll need to recreate a timeline and think of everyone you saw come or go into the room."

The idea startled her. "You think the killer was one of the staff?"

"I think we can't assume or dismiss a thing. You know this will become a high-profile case." The doctor put a hand to her forehead, as if to slow her spinning mind. "A murder, committed right here at the hospital? In our ER, no less! We can't afford to mess this up. Everyone and everything will be suspect."

"Including the three of us," Laurel realized. "We attended to her. I was the last person to see her alive." The last thought was particularly sobering.

"No, the killer was the last person to see her alive," the doctor stated emphatically. Laurel appreciated the vote of confidence. "But you're right. Your boyfriend probably shouldn't be assigned to this case."

"Cade is not my boyfriend," Laurel was quick to point out.

"Have you slept with him?"

"No!" Not that it's anyone's business. But still no.

"Have you kissed him?"

"Well... yes. But—"

The doctor put up a staying hand. "No buts. He'll be biased."

Laurel snorted at the notion. "You obviously don't know Detective Cade Resnick. He's a true professional. I have no doubt he can compartmentalize his personal life from his professional life. Our relationship—whatever it may or may not be—will have no bearing on this case."

"Perhaps not, but the press will see it differently."

Danni nodded in agreement with the doctor. "Remember the circus surrounding Dr. Fisk's death last fall," she reminded her friend.

"I'd rather not. However, I do see your point. And for that reason, I won't call him." She bit back the urge to add, *even though everything inside me is screaming, 'Call Cade!'*

"I think our first line of action is to call Director Gaines. *After* we get the night watchman in here."

"Maybe I should find him and tell him in person," Danni suggested, "rather than blurt it over the intercom."

"Good idea. Laurel and I will stay here until he arrives. Assuming the killer is one of us—" the doctor visibly shivered at the thought— "we don't want to alert him or her that we're suspicious. We need to handle this as discreetly as possible, for everyone's sake. We don't want our other patients to become alarmed."

Danni slipped from the room with a pale face.

"It could have been a visitor," Laurel thought aloud, hoping that were the case. "Someone could have come in with another patient or snuck in when no one was watching."

"As you know, the door won't open without a card. A visitor accompanying a patient is more plausible, but not likely. How would they even know the professor was here? At any rate, we'll let Officer Cho decide the best way to handle visitors."

Laurel blew out a weary sigh. "When I predicted this would be a long night, I had no idea it would include a murder."

The curtain parted, and Nurse Winslow started into the room. He drew up short when he saw the two women already inside.

"Nurse Winslow!" Surprised to see him, Laurel's voice came out more sharply than she intended. She cleared her throat and tried again. "What are you doing in here?"

"I, uh, wanted to make certain the body was presentable. For, uh, the family," the nurse stuttered. He darted his eyes nervously to the prone figure upon the bed. "I believe they're on their way."

"Thank you, but we're taking care of that," the doctor assured him.

"Very well. I'll go back to the floor." He glanced again at the body, before ducking out of the room.

Dr. Ainsley waited a moment before whispering, "Did that seem odd to you?"

"*He* seems odd to me," Laurel admitted. "But surely, our nerves are getting the best of us. We can't honestly suspect one of our nurses." A worry line creased her forehead. "Can we?"

"Like I said before. At this point, no one is above suspicion." The doctor reached out a kind hand and touched Laurel's arm. "I pay my hairstylist to hide them, but there's a lot of gray in this head. I've been in this business far longer than you, my dear. I've seen the best and the worse of mankind. I've seen the things people can do to each other, sometimes to people they love and supposedly cherish. It may sound jaded, but I've learned that no one is a saint. And more people than you can imagine have the capacity to commit a murder."

Laurel nodded. "I've seen it for myself," she confessed, her voice resigned. "That doesn't make it any easier to accept."

"We'll get through this, but we need to remain vigilant. Despite what I just said, I have no doubt about your innocence. You must know, however, that not everyone will see it that way. As you said, you were the last person known to see the patient alive. The police, the press, and the hospital administrators are sure to question that."

Laurel drew in a deep breath and squared her shoulders. "And I'll answer. I have nothing to hide."

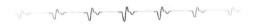

Within the hour, a police presence moved in. They kept it low key, in deference to other patients and to the killer who possibly still roamed among them. Plain-clothes officers posed as patients in the waiting room, watching for any suspicious comings and goings. A uniformed officer took the place of the night watchman outside Room 6, but such a sighting wasn't uncommon, given the local jails in the area. Officers often accompanied prisoners who required medical attention.

The extra traffic and added stress made concentrating difficult, but Laurel dutifully met with Detective Herschel Castilleja and told him everything she could remember concerning the professor. She asked the other nurses to cover for her while she retreated to a vacant waiting room on the second floor. With blessed silence around her, she recreated a timeline and jotted down every person she remembered seeing in or around the patient's room. Already, her memory had grown fuzzy with exhaustion. She doubted a few of her recollections, marking out names only to add them again as she recalled a definite sighting.

Her phone rang just before two a.m., flashing Cade's number across her screen.

"Hello?" She kept her voice low, mindful of the slumbering patients around her.

His voice rough with sleep, Cade didn't bother with a greeting. "Is it true?" he asked.

"I'm afraid so."

"Why didn't you call me?"

"I wanted to call, but we decided it was better if I didn't."

"Who's we?"

"My superiors, for one. We can't afford any media sensationalism."

"You do know that's impossible, right?" He all but snorted. "You remember Dr. Fisk?"

"Yes, but he was the CEO of our biggest competitor, not to mention the husband of your former boss, the College Station Assistant Chief of Police."

"Yes, but Ylenia Tonchev, a newly naturalized citizen of our country, was an esteemed member of the Texas A&M University faculty, and she was apparently murdered while under the care of *Texas*

General. If that doesn't make for a media storm, I don't know what does."

Laurel dropped her forehead against her palm. "What a mess."

"I asked for the case," Cade told her in a low voice, "but Chief Moore denied me. He said I was too close to the situation, and it could be a possible conflict of interest."

"I heard the same thing on my end, but I assured them that wasn't the case. I know you're a consummate professional."

"That's true, but I may have to agree with the chief on this one."

"Really? I'm surprised to hear you say that." Laurel made the statement without thinking.

"Why would that surprise you?" His voice turned sharp, like he took offense with her words.

"We aren't... I mean, we've never... You've never..." She gave up with a sigh. "I'm exhausted. I can't even think straight. Can we pick this up at another time? I need to get back downstairs." She collected her things as she spoke and started down another long hallway.

"Where are you?"

"On the second floor where it's nice and quiet, headed for the back elevators. I'm making a list of potential persons of interest for Detective Castilleja."

"Chel's a good man. He'll do a thorough job on the investigation," Cade assured her.

Thinking she heard footsteps behind her, Laurel turned to peer into the shadowy hall beyond.

With no patients and no testing being performed along the back hall, the lights were dimmer than normal.

When she didn't answer right away, Cade asked, "Laurel? Are you still there?"

"Uhm, yeah. Yeah, I'm here."

"What? You don't agree about Herschel?"

"What? No. No, that's not it."

"What is wrong with you, then? You sound distracted."

"I thought... never mind what I thought." She shook her head at her own foolishness. "Not only am I exhausted, but my nerves are also on edge." She stepped into the elevator and pressed the down button. When the doors were securely shut, she elaborated, "Like Dr. Ainsley and the officers pointed out, we can't rule out the possibility that this was the work of one of our own. It's disconcerting, thinking a killer may work among us. I guess I'm just jumpier than normal."

"Should I come down there?" She loved the sound of his voice when it slipped an octave, wrapping around her like a warmed blanket.

Bad analogy, she realized. It brought to mind Professor Tonchev. If only I had taken the blanket in sooner! I might have saved her life!

"You're doing it again," Cade accused. "You're zoning out. I'll get dressed and be right down."

"No! No, seriously. Don't. They're right. It would only make the situation worse right now. Besides, they're keeping a low profile. Not only because of the patients..." Her voice trailed off as the elevator doors opened.

"I get it. You don't want to alert the killer you're on to him or her in case it is a staff member."

"Exactly."

"I know you're smart enough to know this but be careful. Watch your back."

Her voice almost broke. "I hate this, Cade. Suspecting my friends and co-workers."

"I know, Lovely Laurel. It's a crazy world we live in."

A new surge of concert goers and the after-party crowds had invaded the emergency room. Laurel bit back a groan. "I've got to go. We're swamped."

"Call me when you leave? As in the minute you step through the hospital doors?"

"You really think it's necessary?"

"I'm not taking any chances. Call me." He made it an order.

For once, Laurel was too tired to argue with him. "Fine. I'll call. Until then, go back to sleep. Catch a few hours for me while you're at it."

Of one thing she was certain. There would be no stolen naps on this midnight shift.

Two drunken injuries, one gall bladder attack, and two false heart attacks later, Laurel found a moment to rest. With the police still using the break room to question staff and set up a command post, breaks were relegated to the nurses' stations or other areas of the hospital.

Too tired to seek comfort on the second floor, Laurel took her fifteen in the middle of the action. She pulled out her half-wilted salad, made a cup of coffee, and propped her feet up the best she could while attempting to tune out the world.

"Looks delish," Boomer smirked as he dropped into a chair beside her. It strained under his weight and rolled backward, but it held him upright. The gentle giant seemed not to notice. "Man, what a night!"

"My sentiments, exactly."

"Where's your cowboy? I thought he'd be all over this." He motioned toward the sequestered break room.

"My cowboy?" Laurel pretended not to understand, even though most of her co-workers, despite her claims otherwise, believed the two of them were an item. "If you're referring to Detective Resnick, he's not my anything."

"Really?" When an eager light lit his eyes, Laurel realized the error of her ways. "Because I heard the two of you were going out."

She was torn between sparing Boomer's feelings and sparing unwanted rumors. Boomer was a nice guy, after all, but she hated to give him false hope. Despite her ardent denial, she was already falling for the calf-roping, spur-spangled cowboy detective. On the other hand, she didn't want to admit to a relationship that didn't technically exist, particularly when she never knew who might overhear their conversation. She tried playing it down the middle.

"We've, uh, had a date or two," she admitted. "Nothing serious."

"Still, I figured he was the type to come riding in on his white horse to rescue the damsel in distress."

Chauvinistic remarks like that always prickled under her skin. A fire flashed in Laurel's hazel eyes. "First of all," she informed him hotly, "I'm not a damsel in distress. No white horse needed, thank you very much. And second of all, there's nothing to save me from. I don't even know what all that's about."

"Really?" He cocked his head to one side, allowing his sandy-brown hair to fall into his eyes. "You don't know what that's all about?" He sounded skeptical.

"Routine questions, as far as I can tell," she fibbed with a shrug.

"Doesn't look too routine to me," Boomer said, his tone now thoughtful.

"I think they're just crossing their '*Ts*' and dotting their '*Is*.' Saving themselves from future red tape and all of that." She shrugged again for good measure.

"You think?"

"What else could it be?"

Boomer studied her through narrowed eyes, as if he suspected her of withholding juicy gossip. "You'd tell me, wouldn't you, if you knew something?"

Laurel spread her hands wide and offered him her best smile. "But if I don't, I can't."

Satisfied with her answer, he leaned back in the chair, eliciting a groaned protest from its springs. "So, if you and the cowboy aren't an item, what about catching an Aggie game with me?"

Laurel had never been so happy to see Trevor Winslow as she was at that moment. He had come from behind without her knowing it, and now he snorted in disgust.

"If you two are through flirting with one another, we have a patient waiting in Room 7. *Some* of us would like a chance to get off our feet, too."

Looking unfazed by the gibe, Boomer grinned up at the angry man. "I never took you for the jealous type, Winslow. If I'm stepping on your toes here, just say the word."

The male nurse rolled his eyes in disgust. "Oh, *please*," he huffed, clearly insulted. "As if I'd ever stoop so low."

Laurel was more angered than she was insulted. He could at least attempt hiding his disdain for her.

Rather than show her anger, Laurel brushed it off and made it sound like amusement. "So low as to try dating your superior-ranking nurse? Is that what you meant?" She stood and gave him a patronizing pat on the back. She adopted a British accent. "Good form, old chap. I didn't peg you for such a professional."

She felt the heat from his glare as she exited the nurses' station, five minutes before her break was up.

Ah, there's the scornful glare I've come to know and hate. I don't know the man's story, but he definitely has some anger issues, particularly where women with authority are concerned. I've noticed the same thing with the female doctors on staff.

She drew in a deep, cleansing breath. *And that, as they say, is entirely enough about that. I've put too much thought and energy into Trevor Winslow for one night, as it is. With any luck, I can avoid him for the rest of the shift and not see or think of him again until Tuesday.*

The temperamental man would be off tomorrow night, and then it was Laurel's turn for three full days of leisure. Their schedules wouldn't collide again until Tuesday morning.

Four days without him sounded almost too good to be true.

CHAPTER THREE

As promised, Laurel called Cade at twenty-six minutes after seven. She hit the dial button as she stepped into a day that was deceptively bright and sunny.

"Did you have troubles?" he asked on the first ring.

"Troubles? Of course not. I'm just now leaving."

"I thought your relief got there before seven."

"She does, but we had a lot to go over. I had to catch her up to speed on—" she glanced around, suspicious of her surroundings "—the situation."

"No breakthroughs on the case, I hear."

"None that they're telling us about, at any rate."

She heard someone call her name from behind.

"Hey, Laurel! Wait up."

A sinking sensation stirred in her stomach as Laurel turned to see Boomer rushing her way. "Play along," she hissed through the phone to Cade.

Forcing a smile she didn't feel, she motioned to her phone while giving Boomer an apologetic look.

He caught up with her, seemingly unconcerned to be listening in on her private conversation. He strolled alongside her until she had no choice but to continue speaking into the receiver. "Anyway, Mom, I'm not sure what to tell you about this week. My schedule is pretty jam packed."

"Mom, is it?" Cade asked, sounding mildly amused. He pitched his voice unnaturally high and played along as requested. "Why, dear? What's going on?"

In spite of herself, Laurel burst out laughing. The manly detective sounded ridiculous!

Beside her, Boomer looked puzzled, which only widened her grin.

"Yes, ma'am," she went on, "I've got a crazy-busy schedule this week. Not a minute of downtime." She added this for Boomer's benefit. A peek at the Aggie baseball schedule told her the boys in maroon had two more home games scheduled the coming week, and she wasn't taking a chance on Boomer inviting her to one.

"That doesn't sound right, dear," Cade squeaked. "I thought you were off this week."

"Change of plans. Hang on a minute, Mom, while I tell a friend goodbye. Hold on. I'll be right back." She put her hand over the mic and offered Boomer a distracted smile. "Bye, Boomer. Hope you get some rest today." She gave him no chance to reply as she went back to her conversation. "Okay, I'm back. And you? What's your week like?"

Boomer wavered with indecision for a moment, but he finally got the hint and waved goodbye, wandering off toward a beefed-up Ford truck at the back of the parking lot. Laurel didn't give up the charade until she was tucked inside her own vehicle with the engine running.

"Want to tell me what that was all about?" Cade asked in his normally pleasant baritone.

"Fending off an unwanted invitation to an Aggie baseball game."

"Not one of the Curly Girls, I take it?"

"Nope, not Danni or Cami." The three naturally curly haired best friends made up the trio he referred to.

"An unwanted admirer, then?" he pressed.

"Something like that."

"So, you've taken to beating them off with a baseball bat, have you?"

"Didn't you hear me? I'm hoping it won't come to that."

A warm note slipped into his voice. Laurel dared not classify it as possessive. "Tell him you're already seeing someone."

"But am I? I've hardly spoken to you since our dinner at the Montgomery Ranch." Weariness allowed a whine to accompany her words. By the time even she heard it, it was too late to withdraw. "I'm sorry. Ignore me. I'm exhausted and clearly need my sleep."

"I think that's more than exhaustion in your voice."

"Maybe, but I'm honestly too exhausted to discuss it right now."

"Can you drive home, or do I need to come get you?"

"I'm fine. Already pulling out of the parking lot."

"Perfect. I'm waiting for you at your house."

"What? Why? I told you, I need—"

"—your sleep," he interrupted, finishing her sentence for her. "I get it. I don't plan to come in. I don't even have to get out of my car. I just want to make sure you get home safely."

"Cade, surely you don't think someone will follow me home!"

"I don't, but it never hurts to show extra vigilance."

Something about his smooth reply irked her. He was either patronizing her or protecting her, treating her like the infernal damsel in distress. Either scenario made her angry, especially when she was mentally, physically, and emotionally exhausted.

"I'll make a quick walk through and flash my front light. No need to get out of your car," she told him frostily.

"No need for the walk through. I've been sitting in front of your house since we talked this morning. You're good to go in and go straight to bed."

Laurel bit back a bitter retort about where he could go. In truth, she was incredibly touched that he cared enough to spend the better part of the night staking out her house. So touched that a lump formed in her throat and tears threatened to fall. That, in itself, made her even angrier. She had been fighting the tears all night, and she had no intentions of giving in to them now. Not in front of Cade, and not when she was mere blocks from home and a good five hours of uninterrupted sleep. Crying made her nose stuffy and kept her from sleeping well.

"Laurel? Are you still there?"

She swallowed down the lump and forced out a weak response. "Thanks, Cade. I plan to do just that."

Which, of course, she didn't.

She took one look at the handsome detective sitting patiently in his car, and it was all she could do to wave, unlock her front door, and stumble inside before the tears fell. She cried all through her shower and her meager bowl of cereal, and she was still sniffling as she crawled into bed.

She slept fitfully, her nose stuffed, her eyes swollen, and her heart bruised from not only losing a patient, but losing yet another piece of her heart to one highly infuriating, impossibly charming, but undeniably gallant detective in spurs.

After tossing and turning for at least an hour, Laurel got up earlier than planned. She couldn't summon enough energy to do a load of laundry, but she managed to scramble some eggs and pack a lunch for tonight's shift. She turned on the television to catch the early local news, which was filled with reports of Professor Ylenia Tonchev's unexpected death. So far, no details were released about cause of death, but they did say she had died at a local hospital after calling 911 during an asthma attack.

"I'm sure the vultures will get wind of the details and circle soon," Laurel muttered. "Station WXYZ out of Houston has a knack for these things."

She didn't see Cade's car outside her house when she left for the hospital, but she had a feeling he was nearby. Unwilling to confirm her suspicions and deal with another lumpy throat, she didn't call to ask his whereabouts. But she *sensed* someone following her, even though the sensation left her oddly uncomfortable.

Nerves, she determined. The idea of needing police protection has me rattled.

Without a police presence at the hospital, it was almost possible to pretend things were normal.

Almost, but not quite. There was still the small matter that someone had strangled the professor. That someone was still unknown, and quite possibly one of their own.

It was unnerving, suspecting her friends and co-workers of committing a heinous crime. Laurel couldn't help but look at them differently now, wondering who among them was even capable of such. Perhaps the most puzzling of all was the *why*?

Why would someone want to kill the professor? She taught world literature. Why would someone here want to kill a literary professor?

Tonight was much quieter than the night before, giving Laurel plenty of time to mull the question over in her mind. With few patients demanding her attention, she thought of a dozen possible scenarios, but none seemed to fit.

Someone was working on a master's degree and taking her class. She gave the person a low test score, so he or she retaliated.

But with murder? It was definitely a far reach.

Okay, so perhaps it made their GPA dip low enough to threaten their scholarship.

Or maybe, Laurel considered, the student wasn't someone who worked here. Maybe the student was someone's child. That person could be close to retirement and depending on the scholarship to get their child through college. Without it, they would have to continue working.

But who, she wondered, *could that be?* It would have to be one of their older staff members, still strong enough and agile enough to hold Ylenia Tonchev down to strangle her.

Strangulation wasn't an easy way to kill a person unless that person was unconscious or incapacitated. When Laurel left the professor, she was weakened but certainly capable of fighting back.

It was bad enough suspecting her younger co-workers; to suspect her elders was even worse.

Didn't they deserve a certain level of respect? It didn't absolve them from crime, certainly, but wasn't it wrong of her to create unfounded scenarios in which they were guilty?

In some ways, Laurel understood Trevor's aversion to young leadership. It was almost an insult to older, more experienced workers. She realized that older staff members were often overlooked for promotions simply because of their age, assuming they were 'past their prime' and not up to the task. She knew sometimes the jobs they deserved went to younger, less qualified employees.

Laurel also knew that, age aside, not all employees were leadership material. Trevor was a prime example. She understood he had come to *Texas General* after being overlooked for a promotion at another hospital. That told her he was prideful and thought only of what was best for him personally, and not what was best for the situation at hand. Despite his years of experience, his quick temper, surly attitude, and bouts of open contempt told her that he was too arrogant and too outspoken to be an effective leader.

Maybe I should consider who is physically capable of strangling the professor. She was small but appeared to be well-toned and in good shape. Overpowering her couldn't have been easy. She may have even fought back. Laurel glanced down at her own hands, free of scratches and tell-tale scrapes. Had the detectives examined everyone's hands and arms yesterday? Had the same thoughts occurred to them?

Of course, silly, she chided. They're professionals. They're trained to think and look for such. Now you sound as arrogant as Trevor!

That thought sobered her. Laurel set aside her scenarios and speculations and concentrated on her own area of expertise: nursing. And just in time for a new patient.

"Hello. My name is Laurel, and I'll be your nurse while you're here. What brings you in to the ER tonight?"

"It's so silly, really," the woman on the bed said, hands fluttering around her chest. "I feel so foolish."

Laurel smiled. "If everyone came in each time they felt foolish, we'd never have a free room. Surely there's something more specific we can help you with."

"Yes, of course. I just... I don't know where to start."

"How about you tell me your name?"

Amid nervous laughter, the woman patted her chest again, her cheeks flushed. "Dawn. Dawn Dyson."

"As is Dawn Dyson, Dreams Realtor?" Laurel asked.

The woman was practically a celebrity. Her commercials ran on television and radio networks, and billboards all over the twin cities boasted her name and likeness. It seemed she was everywhere, and all at once.

Laurel peered more closely at the woman on the bed. Up close, she bore little resemblance to the confident woman on the television screen or high in the sky. She detected a few similarities, but apparently Dawn Dyson employed excellent makeup artists and digital designers. The woman on the bed looked older, frailer, and much less certain of herself.

"That would be me," the patient confirmed. "But please. Call me Dawn."

"Very well, Dawn. Can you tell me if you're in any sort of pain? Are you injured somewhere?"

Laurel ran her perfected but less-than-scientific 'ailment assessment' gaze over the woman. Mid to late fifties, perhaps early sixties. Gray hair, covered by a platinum rinse. Pale skin from spending too many hours inside. Poor muscle tone reaffirms that assumption, even though she's slender and appears agile. Seems unusually nervous but could be the setting. ERs have a way of doing that to people. No drug tracks, no obvious signs of use or substance abuse. Mild swelling in right ankle. Could be edema, could be a slight sprain. Overall, in moderate to good health.

"My pride took a definite hit," Dawn admitted. "Tangling your own feet has a tendency to shatter self-confidence."

"You fell and twisted your ankle?" Laurel guessed.

"Yes, exactly! How did you know?"

"Lucky guess."

Once the hands stopped fluttering, Laurel noticed grass stains and small scrapes along both palms.

"Does this hurt?" she asked, gingerly touching the woman's ankle.

"No."

"This?"

"Not really."

Laurel turned her ankle inward, and the woman winced. When she manipulated it into a gentle rotation, Dawn cried out in pain.

"Yes! That hurts!"

"I'm sure the doctor will want to take pictures of this. For now, let's take a look at your palms. It looks like you scraped them before you caught yourself." More to make conversation than anything else, Laurel moved about, gathering supplies, asking over her shoulder, "How did you fall?"

"Again, it was so silly. Nothing, really."

"*Nothing* rarely lands you in the emergency room."

"I was, uh, looking at a piece of property."

"A potential sale?" Again, she asked more out of politeness than any real interest. *Who moved the gauze?* Someone had come in and rearranged the cabinets.

"I hope so, but it's too soon to say. The owner, uh, just recently passed away."

Maybe that's why she seems so nervous. Nothing like doing a little grave robbing. I guess that's what separates her from the amateurs. Her back still turned to the patient, Laurel knew her face might reflect her thoughts.

Instead of voicing her opinions, she asked questions. "How long ago did this happen? Has the swelling lessened, or gotten worse?"

"It's just now swelling. I'd say it happened a good hour and a half ago."

Laurel tried to hide her surprise. It was now close to midnight. Who viewed potential sale properties that late at night?

Catching a glimpse of guilt on Dawn's face, Laurel knew the answer. *Someone who was snooping, that's who!* That's why the woman was so flustered. She was snooping where she didn't belong, fell over something in the dark, and injured herself. Laurel refused to acknowledge the little voice in the back of her head hissing, *Serves her right!*

"This may sting a little," Laurel cautioned as she took one palm and cleaned it. The realtor drew in a sharp breath but never uttered a sound.

"This one isn't so bad. Dab some anti-bacterial ointment on it two to three times a day, and you should be fine. Now for the other one..." She examined the deeper gash on this hand. "Hmm," she said. "This one looks a little worse for wear. Did you fall on something sharp?"

"It was dark. I couldn't see very well. There, uh, may have been something sharp in the flower bed."

That could explain the little leaf I see poking from your hair, Laurel mused. You were poking around in the flower beds, trying to see into the windows!

"This will definitely hurt. That scrape is rather deep."

Dawn cried out in pain, but she didn't jerk away. Laurel cleaned it the best she could, applied ointment and a non-stick pad, and wrapped it well with gauze binding. "You'll need to change the wrappings once a day. Clean and doctor the wound each time with the solution and ointment I'm sending home with you."

"Thank you. I—I feel so foolish."

Keeping her thoughts to herself, Laurel offered a noncommittal smile. "The doctor should be in any mo—"

Before she could finish, Monica Ainsley called out, "Knock, Knock!" and swept into the room.

"Ah, right on cue." Laurel smiled. "Dawn, this is Dr. Ainsley. You're in good hands now."

Surprise registered on the patient's face. "Monica! What are you...? I had no idea you were a doctor here at *Texas General*! I assumed you worked at one of the larger hospitals in town."

"No. I like the nice, cozy feel of *Texas General*," Monica Ainsley replied with a smile. "What brings the number one realtor in Bryan-College Station in this evening? Did you see your latest commission check and get lightheaded with joy?"

"Hardly that." Dawn laughed, although it sounded strained. "I, uh, was viewing a potential property, and I fell. Scraped my palms and twisted an ankle."

"Superficial cuts and scrapes on both palms," Laurel elaborated, "but one gash on her right hand required bandaging. As long as she keeps it clean, it shouldn't pose a problem."

"Very well. Let's take a look at the ankle. This right one, I see."

"Yes, it's rather— ouch! That hurts."

"Let's send her for imaging," the doctor instructed Laurel. "I want a three view of her right ankle." To the patient, she asked, "Anything else hurt?"

"Besides my pride? I think that's all."

As the doctor poked and prodded in a few more spots, she made small talk. "I don't suppose you've found any houses I would be interested in, have you?"

"As a matter of fact..." Dawn Dyson's eyes lit with pleasure. Or maybe it was the calculation of her newest commission; Laurel wasn't certain which. The agent slid a sly look toward the doctor and gushed, "The property I saw tonight would be perfect for you!"

"I'm clumsy enough without any hazardous spots around my house," Dr. Ainsley claimed, looking skeptical. "Does it hurt when I do this?"

"No."

"This?"

"Not at all."

A CASE OF STRANGULATION by A Stranger

"Where is this house? If I'm still alert and conscious when I get off, I might swing by and take a look."

"It's... not exactly on the market," the realtor admitted. "Yet. But I'm certain it will be soon." She sounded confident.

"How many bedrooms?"

"Two beds, two baths, small yard. A large kitchen and walk-in closets, just like you want. And exactly in that highly sought-after neighborhood you favored." Dawn Dyson offered her best saleswoman smile. "You only *thought* there were no houses available there!"

Laurel looked up in surprise. "You're selling your house?"

"It's just Robert and me now," Dr. Ainsley explained. "We don't have any grandchildren, and our sons have places of their own. We're hoping to downsize. Dawn is looking for a suitable house for us to buy before we put ours on the market."

"Yours is so gorgeous, it should sell in no time," Laurel agreed. She had attended a Christmas party there over the holidays.

"That's why we want to find a place to go first, so we don't find ourselves out on the streets. Dawn, we'll get those images, and then we'll talk. I need you healthy and mobile, so you can show me around this great house you found."

"I'd love to!" Dawn beamed.

The doctor left as Laurel finished with her patient. "I didn't realize Robert and Monica were selling their house. Have you seen it? It has a great layout."

"Yes, I have no doubt we can get top dollar for it. And this new property will be perfect for them. If I didn't know better, I would think she had selected it herself! All I have to do is get the listing, and we'll all come out winners."

"Except for the previous owner," Laurel pointed out. "Didn't you say he had recently passed away?"

"She," the realtor corrected. "And yes, quite recently. Yesterday, actually."

An uneasy feeling moved through Laurel. Perhaps it was surprise.

"And the house is already going on the market?" she asked.

"Not officially. But once I speak to the family, explain what it's worth, and that I already have an interested buyer, they may decide to list it. I understand the professor wasn't married."

"The—The professor?"

"Yes, the one who passed away yesterday. I'm sure you saw it on the news. That pretty one from Bosnia. Or was it Belgium? One of the B countries."

"Bulgaria," Laurel murmured.

"Yes, I believe that was it. Apparently, she suffered an asthma attack. Luckily, it wasn't in her home." The realtor never noticed how quiet her nurse had become as she prattled on. "It's silly, really, but people don't like to live in houses where someone has died. It gives the house an unnecessary stigma, even though it's hardly the home's fault! I believe the news says she passed away at an area hospital, which means her home won't lose any of its value. All the better for me. And for her poor, grieving family, of course," she added.

"Of course." Laurel gathered her supplies and vowed to never watch another Dawn Dyson Dreams Realtor commercial again. "A tech will be in shortly for those images."

CHAPTER FOUR

The rest of the night was relatively quiet. When Cade texted to say he was sitting in her driveway, her only reply was that they would talk later. With the next three days off, she only needed a few hours' sleep in order to function until nightfall.

By early afternoon, she was up and puttering around the house. She gathered her laundry from the last few days and sorted colors at the washing machine.

Knowing she was bad about forgetting to empty her pockets, Laurel checked them all now. She unintentionally turned one set of shrubs upside down and heard the metallic clink of something falling into the washer's tub.

"What did I leave in there this time?" she muttered, hoisting herself up on her tiptoes to reach the bottom of the tub. What had she been thinking, buying such a tall washing machine? Arm buried up to her shoulder, she fished around blindly, expecting a quarter or a fountain pen.

When something cold and thin slithered in and out of her palm, she all but squealed. *Lizards and snakes don't sound like metal, genius,* she told herself sternly. She made another swipe, snagged the unseen item, and pulled it out.

"Hmm. A necklace. I wonder where this came from. I don't think I've ever seen it before." She turned it over in her hand, examining the pendant hanging from a thick rope chain. "A little chunky for my tastes," she murmured, "but pretty. Wonder how it ended up here?"

The necklace offered no clues. With a shrug, Laurel slipped it into her jeans pocket. Maybe it belonged to one of the other nurses at the hospital and somehow fell into the large pockets of her scrubs. It was the only explanation she could think of.

She added her clothes and detergent, and then turned the machine on. Her phone buzzed as she closed the door to the washroom.

"You up?" Cade asked.

"Good thing," she said, "or you would have woken me."

"Are you up for dinner tonight?"

"I don't feel like Mexican food."

The detective sounded offended. "You really think the only place I'll take you is *Mama G's Tacqueria*? I had something nicer in mind. Maybe the steak house where we had dinner with Brash and Madison?"

"I'm not sure I feel like going out anywhere tonight. It's been a tough couple of days."

"Are you avoiding me?" he asked, point blank.

She didn't answer directly. "I don't feel like dressing up tonight. I was hoping for a quiet night in."

"We can do that," he said, not giving up so easily. "I can bring a couple of steaks or fish to throw on the grill, or I can bring takeout. Your choice."

"I can cook something," she said, but her tone was less than enthusiastic.

"Like you said, it's been a tough couple of days. Let me bring something. What sounds good?"

"Coming off the night shift, nothing too spicy," she requested.

"I know how much you like *Layne's* chicken fingers."

"I should have never told you my weakness. How about I make a big salad to go with them, and we'll pretend we're eating healthy?"

He chuckled and agreed. "Sounds good. Seven-ish?"

"Not too *ish*-y," she warned. "I'm coming off the night shift, remember? I'd like to make it through dinner without falling asleep."

With a chuckle, Cade amended the time. "Seven on the dot."

"See you then."

Laurel grudgingly noticed that her spirits lifted after the phone call. Funny, what the thought of chicken fingers did for a gal's esteem.

"Yeah," she muttered aloud as she tucked the phone into her pocket. "You keep telling yourself that. It's just the chicken fingers. Nothing to do with the hot man delivering them."

Theirs was a complicated relationship. As Laurel straightened things around the house and fluffed her couch pillows, she thought about the past five months since she had known the detective. More than once, they had clashed over their careers. Laurel was determined to protect her patients and put their health and well-being first, even when they wound up in one of Cade's criminal investigations. They were both dedicated professionals and passionate about what they did, which didn't always bode well for their budding romance.

"Budding?" she questioned herself aloud. "Get real. I think it's gone dormant. A few promising kisses and a couple of dates. A few dinners with friends and one with his parents, even if it was at their own café. Hardly the makings of a grand romance."

She punched the pillow a little harder than necessary. "He goes days without calling. Weeks without darkening my doorstep! Coffee on the go and lunch in the hospital cafeteria now and then. And now, all of a sudden, he acts like we're an item. *'Tell him you're already seeing someone,'* he says." She mimicked him, although her nasal sneer sounded nothing like Cade's deep drawl. "*'You're surprised I would find it a conflict of interest?'*" she continued. Now she was paraphrasing, but she had the general gist. The pillow suffered the brunt of her emotions. "Where's the conflict? More importantly, where's the interest? That's what I want to know! Where's the interest, Cade?"

Realizing what she did to the innocent pillow, Laurel pulled it to her and sank onto the couch. She was clearly overwrought and exhausted on every level. Maybe tonight wasn't the best time to have Cade over.

She called him back and told him so.

"Are you really that tired?" he asked, his voice sounding disappointed but sympathetic.

"Apparently I am. I just had an argument with you in my head."

He found that amusing. "Who won?"

"Clearly not my poor pillow."

Was that a scowl she heard? "You're not making any sense."

"Like I said. It's been a rough couple of days, and I'm running on fumes."

"You obviously need food and are in no condition to cook. I'm bringing dinner."

"I'm not in the best of moods. I might say something I live to regret."

"All the more reason for me to come. It's time we sat down and had a talk."

Great. He's breaking up with me before we even really begin. Can this week get any worse?

"That—That doesn't sound good." She managed to push out the words.

His came out more softly. "It's time we cleared the air between us."

She knew he would only badger her until she heard him out. It was better to end it now, while she still had hopes of a future.

A very bleak, lonesome future.

"Okay," she relented. "Seven o'clock." Hoping to disguise her heartache, she added, "Don't make me wait on my chicken fingers."

Unaware of her broken heart, he chuckled. "Chicken and a bottle of wine, promptly at seven."

She hung up, grumbling to herself. "Who brings wine to break up with a girl? Shows how much he knows. His social skills are even rustier than mine!"

She made a short grocery list while her clothes finished washing. Once they were done, she yanked a brush through her hair, grabbed her purse, and headed out the door. She was almost to her car when a familiar one-ton pickup truck pulled in behind her.

"Hey, Laurel," the sandy-haired giant said.

"Oh, hey, Boomer."

"Going somewhere?"

Hoisting her purse up on her shoulder, she shrugged. "Errands. You know how it is when you finally get a day off."

"I thought you told your mom you were working all week." He narrowed his eyes as if trying to detect a trick.

"No," she hedged. "That's not what I said."

He shook his head stubbornly. "I'm pretty sure that is what you said."

Why are we even having this conversation? She wondered silently. Aloud, she maintained, "I said I was super busy. I have today off. Although, technically, I worked the first seven hours of it, so that may not qualify as a day off."

"You're on the schedule tomorrow?" he asked in surprise.

"No," she admitted. "But I have a ton of things to do."

"Need help with any of them?" His tone was hopeful.

"Sure. You can go to the dentist for me. Let him grind around on your teeth with his drill."

"No, thanks," Boomer said, putting up his hands in surrender. "I'm not too fond of dentists."

"Who is? But they're a necessary evil."

"Necessary evil," he parroted.

An awkward moment stretched between them.

Laurel shifted on her feet, and Boomer jiggled the keys in his pocket.

She felt sorry for the guy. He really was nice. If she weren't involved with Cade, she might even take him up on his offer of going to a game.

You're not involved with Cade, her evil inner voice reminded her. He's breaking up with you tonight.

Yeah, she shot back, but my heart is involved. That's what makes this so hard!

Just as she was about to give in and take mercy on the guy, he spoke up. "I was going to see if you had changed your mind about that game, but it sounds like you're pretty busy. Maybe another time?"

She hated to give him false hope. On the other hand, if tonight went the way she expected, she could use a friend in the future. "Yeah, maybe so," she agreed, her tone just a little too bright.

"So, I guess I'll go..."

She knew her response was lame. She waved vaguely toward her car. "Yeah. I have those errands."

He backtracked down the driveway. "Good luck at the dentist."

"If you change your mind about taking my place..."

"I won't," he assured her.

This time, her response was sincere. She even laughed a little. "I don't blame you!"

He looked so sad, walking backwards toward his truck. Her heart went out to him.

"I'd invite you in, but I have those errands..."

"Another time."

"Sure. Another time."

Laurel threw her purse into her car, her body not far behind. "Well, that was awkward," she groaned. She guilelessly gave credit where credit was due. "Cade Resnick, you are wrecking my life!"

Her mood hardly improved with her grocery outing. Of all the people to run into at the store, Laurel ran into Trevor. Literally. Their buggies collided as they rounded the same corner from opposite directions.

"What?" he spat. "It's not enough to ruin my day at work? Now you have to invade my days off?"

"I'm hardly *invading* you," she argued. "Normally, I try to avoid you."

"You do a pathetic job of it. It seems like every time I round a corner—like now—there you are."

"Look, Trevor. I don't know what your problem is, but—"

"*You* are my problem! You and all the other women like you."

"And here I was, thinking I was unique," she mumbled.

"No, you think you're cute. You think you can toss your hair or your hips, and that men will just fall at your feet to do your bidding. But I got news for you, toots. It don't work like that."

For one wild moment, Laurel was tempted to give it a try. She could toss her hair, wiggle her hips, and watch him fall to the ground. Then she would stomp on him, twisting her foot just so...

Shaking herself from her fantasy, Laurel proposed a less satisfactory solution, but one that might just work. "Why don't we just pretend to get along and avoid each other at all costs?"

"One problem. You still fancy yourself my superior."

"Not true. But I do outrank you. If you have a problem with it, you should take it up with both of our superiors. Again," she added, knowing he had already complained on previous occasions.

"If I thought it would do any good, believe me, I would. Right now, all anyone can think about is how to spin a positive light on Professor Top Chef's death."

"*Who?*"

He quickly corrected his slip. "Professor Tonchev. Who did you think I was referring to? Has there been another death I'm unaware of?" he asked snidely.

"I imagine so, but none that I know of at the ER."

"So last night was fairly quiet?"

His change of attitude came out of nowhere, but Laurel decided to go with the flow. She suspected the man was bipolar, but she could play nice.

"Not too bad."

"What doctors were on?"

"Ainsley and Peters."

"Is Peters new? I don't know that name."

"He does a rotation with us about once every three months. I think he's out of Brenham."

"Did you think Ainsley was acting odd the other night?"

Laurel shifted on her feet. "Odd?"

"Yeah. All suspicious and hush-hush. Odd. Even more so than she normally is," he clarified.

"I don't guess I noticed. There was a lot going on." The first sentence was a borderline lie. The second was one hundred percent truth.

"Do the police know anything else about the professor's death?" Trevor asked.

"If they do, they aren't sharing with us." This, too, was true. She, Danni, and Dr. Ainsley had come to their own conclusions, without input from the police department. "On the bright side," she said, changing the subject, "at least your patient pulled through."

"My patient?" He looked at her blankly, as if he didn't understand her meaning.

"The ambulance patient in 10," she reminded him. "You know. I took the call in 6, you took the ambulance. The guy that almost chopped off his leg with a chainsaw."

"Oh, yeah. Right."

Does he truly not remember? How can he not remember! Laurel tried again. "It was kind of crazy, the way both things happened almost at once."

"Crazy," he agreed, but his eyes were still cloudy. "That's the ER for you."

Laurel pulled her cart free from his and backed warily away. "I guess I'd better get started shopping," she said. She offered a wave of farewell. "Bye."

But all the while, she was thinking, This guy has flipped his lid. He truly has no clue what I'm talking about.

CHAPTER FIVE

Laurel wouldn't allow Trevor to ruin her evening more than it already was. Laurel drove home with that thought ringing in her head.

She opened the door off the carport, backed her way inside, turned around, and let out a startled cry. Her washroom was in total disarray. Clothes had been pulled from the dryer and from the hanging racks overhead, left in a tangled heap on the floor.

Her kitchen was even worse. Every drawer was open and/or overturned. Pots and pans were flung from the cabinets. Even her cleaning supplies lay scattered on the floor beneath her sink.

Laurel knew not to touch anything. She stood still and listened, not hearing movement from within the rest of the house. She dialed Cade's number as she cautiously ventured into the living room.

He answered with a chuckle. "Can't wait till seven?"

"I've been robbed!"

"Wait. What?"

"Someone broke into my house and trashed the placed. Everything is in total chaos." She rubbed her forehead as she looked around the room. "The TV and stereo are still here. Nothing glares at me as having been stolen in the living room, but all the cushions are on the floor. Not slashed, thank goodness. The kitchen was in shambles, but again, nothing visibly missing or broken. I'm moving into the hall."

"You need to get out of there, Laurel! I'm sending a patrol car as we speak."

She only half-heard him speaking into his radio, dispatching a unit to her address. She peered into her bathroom. All the linens were thrown into her vintage claw-foot tub. The medicine cabinet stood ajar, most of the contents swept into the sink below. The drawers of the wicker set beneath the window were upended onto the floor.

"At first glance, nothing is missing. All my electronics, including televisions and computer, are here," she reported, peeking into the rest of the rooms. "They must have been looking for money. Without touching anything, it even appears my jewelry is in place. Not, mind you, that it's worth much beyond sentimental value."

"The intruder could still be in the house, Laurel. You need to wait outside."

"I'm pretty sure the person is gone."

"I don't want you taking any chances. I'll be there in seven minutes."

"You don't have to—"

"I'm on my way. Wait in your car until a squad car or I arrive." He ground out the words, not waiting for her to respond before hanging up the phone.

"Who does he think he is?" she grumbled.

But she did as he asked, needing to escape the mess that her home had become.

Time dragged by. The investigative team was inside doing their thing while two other officers questioned Laurel in the driveway.

Cade arrived in under six minutes. He folded her into a hard, partially hidden embrace before speaking to the officer in charge. Seconds later, he whisked her away to the privacy of his pickup truck.

She told him again what had happened. Rattled by the break in, it was almost easier for Laurel to concentrate on something else. "What have you heard about the murder case?" she asked.

"Not much. I can't decide if it's because they've got nothing, or because they've got something and don't want to tell me about it."

"Has the autopsy come back?" Laurel asked.

"Not officially. For now, they're only saying she choked to death."

Laurel shook her head. "That's not right. I saw the bruising around her neck. She was strangled." When he merely frowned, she went on to explain. "There's a difference. Choking is internal. Something physically blocks air from moving in and out of the trachea or windpipe. Usually there's

BECKI WILLIS

something stuck in the trachea, but sometimes it's lodged in the esophagus, blocking the pipe, and thereby causing an obstruction. Strangulation is external. Something compresses the neck enough to restrict airflow. The trachea is still denied air, but from external pressure."

"I know the difference. What I didn't know was that you saw bruising. Where was it?"

Laurel put her hand up to her throat to demonstrate. "Like this. There was a distinct pressure point on the right side, like a thumb would make, and a line on the left."

"So, the killer was right-handed," he assessed.

"It was the easiest way to access the bed."

"No matter, the killer would use their dominant hand to apply the force needed to strangle someone. It's not as quick and easy as the movies make it look."

"I made the same observation. When I left her, she was alert and able to fight back. Don't get me wrong. She suffered a severe asthma attack, and her lungs were stressed, but she wasn't so weak that she couldn't struggle against an attack. She was hardly in an incapacitated state."

"Unless her attacker rendered her that way."

"Which will show in the autopsy." Laurel nodded. "I'm just now realizing this, but her attacker had to have been familiar with hospital equipment. He or she disengaged the monitors without triggering any alarms. Even if she struggled, it didn't register on the board. There were no signs of elevated heart rate or distress, so no alarms."

"And so no one realized what was happening," Cade observed thoughtfully.

"Plus, there was another emergency on the other end of the hall, almost simultaneously. An ambulance brought in a man who nearly amputated his own leg. At one point, they almost lost him. It was still touch and go with him when I discovered the professor."

"It really was a tough night." A hum of sympathy accompanied his words.

"Not to mention all the typical craziness of a night in the ER." She twisted a dark curl around her finger. "Notice I didn't say 'normal.' I said typical. Nothing about that night was normal."

"There was that big concert in town. I'm sure a lot of college kids went, and I'm sure quite a few wound up in the ER for one reason or another. Did any of them stand out to you? Any of them especially belligerent?"

"Not that I recall. Why?"

"The victim was a college professor. It stands to reason that a student could have held a grudge against her and was just drunk enough, or high enough, to act on his or her grudge."

"Murder seems a bit drastic, but maybe. Even so, most of those didn't come in until after the concert was over. The professor died well before that."

Looking stumped, Cade stared out the windshield at the activity surrounding her house.

She went back to his earlier statement. "Why did you say they may know something but deliberately aren't telling you? What would they know?"

"I have no idea."

When he didn't quite meet her eyes, she got that sinking feeling again. "But you think it might be something concerning me." She made it a statement, not a question.

"Like I told you before. The chief thinks I have a conflict of interest. I'm not part of the case."

"But what would it matter what you knew, unless I was a person of interest?"

Cade kept a poker face, but she felt him tense beside her.

Laurel's eyes widened. "That's it, isn't it? *I'm* a person of interest! But... But that's ridiculous!" She bounced from a question to an exclamation, and then back to a question. A dazed, outraged question. "They think *I* did this?"

"Honestly, Laurel, I have no idea what they think. Like I said, I'm out of the loop. But if it were my case..."

"If it were your case, what?" she demanded. "*You* would suspect me?"

"Not you, per se. But you have to look at it from a detective's standpoint. The last person known to see the victim alive is also the first person to report her dead. You have to admit that's rather odd."

"Obviously, you aren't a health care professional." Laurel sniffed. "It's not nearly as unusual as you seem to think."

"You said it yourself. She didn't simply choke, she was strangled. Whoever did it knew their way around the hospital. We aren't talking about a normal death. This was murder."

"But if you were in charge of the case..." she pressed.

"If I were in charge of the case, I would follow the evidence. I don't have that at my disposal, but from the outside looking in, it would appear you had the opportunity and the means to commit the crime."

"And what would my motive have been?" she challenged.

Cade reached out to still her knee, his hand lingering there. His words were sincere as he looked her in the eye. "*I could never suspect you of murder, Lovely Laurel, no matter how much evidence there might be. That's why the captain didn't give me the case. He knew I wouldn't be objective."

"But—"

"But let the process work," he urged, gently squeezing her knee. "It won't take long for Herschel and the other detectives to come to the same conclusion I've known all along. No matter the circumstances, you could never commit murder."

Before he could say more, his phone buzzed. He was being called back to the office on another case. They had a lead on an ongoing murder investigation he was in charge of.

Wary of curious eyes, Cade squeezed her hand, promised to call the moment he could, and encouraged her to spend the night with her parents or friends.

After Cade was gone and the officers had asked Laurel more questions, one of them accompanied her into the house to gather an overnight bag. It broke her heart seeing her sanctuary violated in such a way, but more than that, it made her angry.

"I can't stand this, Cami," she told her friend as she paced along the floor. With her parents out of town, she called Cami St. John. Her friend was happy to have her for as long as needed. "Someone broke into my house! No locks were jimmied, so they had to have come through a window. Now I have to consider better locks and alarms for all my windows. But far worse than that is the sense that I'm no longer safe in my own home. That's ridiculous! If you aren't safe at home, where are you safe?"

"I know, sweetie," Cami said reassuringly. "It's not right. I'm so sorry this has happened to you."

"Who would do this?"

Cami shrugged her shoulders. "Someone looking for money or drugs, most likely. It could have been a random search of the neighborhood, looking for those one or two houses with easy access and no one at home. Or it could have been someone who knows you're a nurse and thought you might have drugs at your house."

"As if! What do they think I am, a walking pharmacy?"

"People like that don't think. They're just looking for their next fix."

"I live in a quiet, older, historical neighborhood. Most of my neighbors are senior citizens who are home all day. This couldn't be high on the list of *Best Places to Score a Hit in BCS.*" A new thought occurred to her, and she gasped. "I hope my neighbors are okay! Surely, I would have heard if any of them have been robbed or attacked. Poor Mr. Arnie across the street can hardly get around with a walker these days, and the Bates are planning a big trip in their RV. I hope this doesn't discourage them from going."

"I'm sure the police will talk with the neighbors. They'll know if anyone else was a victim."

"You think I was targeted?" As worried as she was about her neighbors, this thought was even more terrifying. "I had just run out for an errand. I was gone less than an hour. Either they're timing was uncanny, or someone was watching and knew my schedule."

"Honestly, it could have been either," her friend pointed out. "Maybe they were cruising the street and saw you leave. It could have been a crime of convenience."

"Or a crime of casing," Laurel mumbled. "Someone may know my schedule. They could be watching my house."

"Who could possibly know your schedule unless they were one of us? I swear, our coordinator doesn't know the schedule half the time! I think she throws a dart or selects names out of a hat. My schedule next week is insane. It's like she's deliberately sabotaging any chance of sleep or social life."

"One—One of us?"

Cami eyed her with suspicion. "Why do you sound like that?"

"Like what?" Laurel asked, avoiding direct eye contact.

"Like you're worried. Almost frightened."

Laurel hesitated as another terrible thought occurred to her.

She had seen Trevor when she first entered the store. His shopping cart had several items inside already. Had he been headed to the checkout counter as she arrived? Had he had enough time to leave the store, drive to her house, ransack the interior, and get handily away while she grocery shopped? It made sense in a weird, Trevor-isque way.

"I, uh... a thought just came to me," she finally confessed. "What if this is connected to Professor Tonchev's death?"

"I don't see how." Her blond-haired friend frowned. "Or why, for that matter. What do you have to do with her death?"

"I found her. There's already a very good chance—I'd guess eighty percent or higher, but that's not an official number—that someone with ties to the hospital killed her. What if the killer thinks I know something? What if, for whatever reason, he or she thinks I could identify them?"

"Then they would already be behind bars," Cami pointed out.

"Not necessarily. Maybe they think the police are still gathering evidence against them so that the charges stick."

"I think you're overwrought with nerves, and justly so," her friend said, gently tugging on her arm. "Come on. Sit down. Relax. Let me pour you a glass of wine to calm your nerves."

Laurel resisted, but not much. "I feel like I should be *doing* something," she countered. With a sigh, she sank into the arms of a nearby chair.

"I'll just be a jiffy," Cami promised, disappearing into the kitchen.

The irony didn't escape her distraught guest. "That's the last thing I said to the professor," Laurel said. "If I hadn't gotten sidetracked, she might still be alive."

With the open floor plan of her apartment, Cami could easily carry on a conversation from the counter separating the two spaces. "How did you get sidetracked?" she asked as she poured wine into two long-stemmed glasses.

"Another patient called for help. He had delayed symptoms of a concussion and could hardly walk back to his room after using the restroom."

"What were you doing for the professor?"

"Getting a warm blanket." Laurel tilted her head and said, "I thought I'd already told you all this?"

"You did. My point is, helping a patient safely back to bed tops getting a warm blanket for one who's already tucked in. You made a judgment call that was spot-on."

"But if I had just carried through with my promise..." Laurel nibbled on her lip with worry as she took the glass handed to her.

"... then the concussed patient could have fallen and seriously hurt him or herself. You can't second guess yourself, Laurel. You did what any nurse would do. Safety before comfort."

Laurel took a sip of wine, pushing the chardonnay to the back of her throat so that the fruity, buttery flavors could awaken her taste buds. The wine slid smoothly down, bringing with it a satisfying sense of comfort. "I suppose," she conceded.

"I highly doubt it had anything to do with the break in. What would be the point?"

"Maybe it was never intended to be a robbery. I can't see where anything was taken, not even my change bowl or piggy bank. Maybe this was intended as a scare tactic."

"Did it work?"

"Am I scared? Yes. Do I know what I'm scared of, other than my own home? No."

"So, what would be the point of ransacking your house, if it has no direct correlation to

Professor Tonchev's death? I honestly can't see where this is related. I think you're grasping at straws."

"Maybe you're right. I guess it doesn't make any sense. It's not like I'm withholding evidence to the police, and a break-in will ensure my silence."

Cami smiled, happy her friend had finally seen things from her perspective. "Exactly. Like it or not, I think this was just one of those random things."

Cami directed the conversation in other areas, but she could see the way Laurel nibbled her lower lip in distraction. The slight tremble in her hand revealed her nervousness. After several minutes, Laurel introduced a new subject, leading with an odd question.

"How well do you know Trevor Winslow?"

The question came out of left field, but Cami furrowed her brow and answered, "I suppose as well as you can know someone after working with them only a few days a week over a period of two or three months. Not well, but enough to establish a rhythm. Why do you ask?"

"Do you think he's... odd?"

Her droll response wasn't really a laugh. "'Odd' doesn't begin to describe that man! Odd, arrogant, and obnoxious are the polite words that come to mind. But for all that, he's also a good nurse. So, I try not to complain whenever we pull a shift together."

"All true," Laurel said, the doubt still lingering in her voice. She placed her empty glass on the table. "Do you ever find him condescending? Like he's superior, simply because he's a man?"

"Without a doubt. The man has a chip on his shoulder the size of Kyle Field. He's convinced he should be the head of the medical world, and anything less is beneath him."

"Has he ever struck you as ... unstable?"

"Sulky, yes. Moody and temperamental, yes. Mercurial, absolutely. But unstable? I'm not sure. Why do you ask?"

"I'm not sure how to describe it. A weird vibe I'm getting, maybe? He came into the professor's room shortly after she was pronounced dead and looked... nervous. Dr. Ainsley and I were in there, so he left abruptly, saying he was just making certain her body was presentable for the family, but he seemed a little unsettled."

"I don't care how often we see it, it's still difficult to stare death in the face," Cami reminded her softly.

"Absolutely, but this felt like more than being uncomfortable in the presence of a dead body. I don't know. It just struck us as odd. And then..." Laurel took a deep breath, steeling herself for an accusation she wasn't certain she should consider. "And then today, I ran into him at the grocery store."

"And?"

"And we had a very odd encounter. It started with hostility, of course. He accused me of running into him on purpose and basically making him miserable by my mere existence. Two minutes later, he was carrying on a normal conversation."

"Bipolar?" Cami mused.

"And then some! But the really odd thing is that when I mentioned a patient he had attended the same day the professor died, he seemed to have no recollection of it. If it were something minor like a strained wrist or heartburn, I could understand. But this was a Code Green that turned into a Level 1 Trauma. A man came in with a chainsaw wound, and Trevor was the attending nurse. They called for a crash cart; that's hardly something you forget."

"Maybe he was ... distracted?"

"Distracted. Drugged. Disoriented. I'm not sure what, but the man had a blank expression on his face when I brought it up. He was clueless."

"That is weird," Cami agreed. "Even for Trevor. But how does that tie into the professor's death?"

Laurel shrugged, suddenly inexplicably exhausted. "Maybe it doesn't. Maybe, like you say, I'm grasping for straws. But the simple truth is that the professor's murder aside, I'm not convinced Trevor isn't just weird enough to have left the store, gone to my house knowing I was away, and trashed the place simply out of spite."

Cami whistled lowly. "That's some accusation. And sadly enough, it doesn't sound entirely impossible." She took a good look at her friend and put out a hand. "Let me help you up. You look dead on your feet. You, girlfriend, are headed to the shower and then to bed. No arguments."

"Not a one," Laurel agreed.

She was just crawling into bed when Cade called.

"I'm sorry about tonight, Laurel. I wanted to stay there with you, but—"

"I know. Your other case. I understand."

"Do you?" He seemed worried she might not understand the position he was in.

"I may not sound like it," she admitted, "but it's the exhaustion speaking. I know a lead on a murder trumps breaking and entering."

"I wanted to be there for you, but you're right. This may be the break we needed to find our killer."

"Is that about the body parts they found in the dumpster?"

"Unofficially?" His tone was guarded.

"Of course."

"Yes. That's the one."

"I don't envy you on that case," she said, shivering at the thought of dismemberment. "I have no idea how someone could do that to another human being."

"Because they aren't human, themselves. They're animals." Cade's voice was harsh. He made a deliberated effort to change his tone with his next words. "But I didn't call to talk about that. I called to say how sorry I was that I couldn't be there for you tonight. I understand they've finished up, and you've gone somewhere else for the night?"

"Cami's. My parents are out of town," Laurel explained.

She heard a smile move into his words. "Can we reschedule the chicken fingers for tomorrow night?"

"Assuming I can put my house back together by then, I think we can manage."

"Would you like to go out instead?"

"No. I'll have a full day tomorrow, cleaning up the mess."

"What about my house? I could pick you up and drive you home. All you have to do is show up and eat."

"How about this?" she suggested. "Let's see how far along I get tomorrow. Call me about six, and I'll update you on my progress."

"Sounds good. One way or another, it's a date," Cade said, his voice affirmative.

"A date," she echoed, sounding less certain than he did.

CHAPTER SIX

The day didn't go well.

The police had released the scene and given her permission to enter, but simply the terminology— 'released the scene'—made Laurel's skin crawl. Her home was now the scene of a crime.

The day was bright and sunny, but a storm cloud hovered over her head and within her heart. Laurel turned on every light in the Craftsman, trying to chase away any hint of lingering shadow. She couldn't quite shake the feeling of something evil hovering in obscurity.

The harsh light made the mess all the more visible. Fine powder shimmered on a multitude of surfaces, mingling with dust particles, and multiplying into a dusty, hazy mess. The leftover residue was another reminder that an intruder had been in her house, potentially leaving fingerprints behind. Dust or not, now *everything* required cleaning.

But first, she must straighten the disorder.

She went through the house, righting overturned chairs and small pieces of furniture. She snagged pillows, afghans, and bed covers from the floor, replaced cushions, folded linens, and threw all her clothes into the laundry room for a wash-day marathon. Laurel could take no chances; the intruder could have touched her undergarments and socks when upending the dresser drawers. She wanted no lingering doubts that her clothes were tainted by hatred and disrespect.

Laurel's dryer couldn't keep up with the many loads of laundry. She resorted to hanging half her wardrobe and most bulky items outside, draped over patio furniture and suspended from hanging pot hooks, the eaves of the porch, and whatever spot she could find. She rigged up a makeshift clothesline to hold towels and sheets. By the second load, the line sagged, and her clean laundry fell to the grass.

As she bent to pluck the items up—*surely, the eight-second rule applied to clothes, not just dropped food*— she had the oddest sensation of being watched. The fine hairs at the back of her neck stood at attention. As discreetly as possible, Laurel glanced around the backyard, unable to find the source of her discomfort. She made fast work of her task, hurried back inside, and locked the door behind her.

Moments later, her phone rang, but no one was on the other end of the line.

Thirty minutes after that, it rang again.

The pattern continued for the next two hours, although she refused to answer after the third attempt. The caller never left a message.

By mid-afternoon, her nerves were shattered. The last thing she needed was to 'clear the air' with Cade.

Taking the coward's way out, she sent him a text.

Sorry, but I don't think tonight will work. Still much to do and already exhausted.

It was a good ten minutes before he replied.

Just as well. I was about to call you. Boss informed me I have other plans tonight. Raincheck?

Laurel sighed as she punched out an answer. Between them, they had enough rainchecks to start a flash flood.

Sure.

Bubbles soon appeared.

Talk to you tonight, Lovely Laurel.

She didn't bother with a reply. Plans and promises could always change.

Tucking the phone away, Laurel headed back into the laundry room for another load. She was derailed when someone knocked on the front door.

Expecting a delivery, she cautiously went to the door and peeked outside. Instead of a brown uniform, she saw a blue-striped pullover stretched across a broad chest and a generous belly. *Boomer.*

Torn between answering and ignoring the intrusion, her Southern manners finally won. Forcing a weak smile, she opened the door. "Boomer. What a surprise." She graciously left out the clarification of 'unwanted.'

"Hey," her unexpected guest said, somewhat shyly. "I, uh, don't mean to intrude, but I heard what happened to you. I wanted to see if you needed any help."

Assuaged by guilt, Laurel opened the door wider. "That's kind of you. Come in." She caught a whiff of cologne as he pushed through the threshold. "How—How did you hear?"

He shrugged his gently sloping shoulders. "Hospital grapevine. You know how it is."

Laurel sighed. "Yes. I do." She waved her arm toward the living room. "It's still a mess, but come on in. Have a seat."

"I'm serious. I came to help, not to visit."

"That's very generous, but I think I have most everything done but the laundry. That may take me a week to finish. And I could use a break. Want to join me in a glass of tea?"

Ever the comic, Boomer pulled a face. "Might get crowded with both of us in there. I'll take a glass of my own if you don't mind."

She couldn't help but shake her head and smile. "Sweet?"

He flashed a boyish grin. "Is there any other kind?"

Laurel made two glasses of iced tea and returned to find her guest roaming about her living room, poking around an antique secretary that held an eclectic mix of her favorites. His chunky fingers moved carefully among her curios on the upper shelves.

"Careful," she warned. "I may have left some of the fingerprint powder. You may draw back inky fingers."

"No problem," he said, brushing his fingers onto his jeans leg. He didn't offer an apology for snooping. He took the glass she offered and waited for her to have a seat before he took his place on the sofa. "So, what happened? They said you were robbed?"

"Yes, although in all honestly, I haven't discovered anything missing yet. I suppose the better term is that I was ransacked."

"Any idea why?" the sandy-haired giant asked, taking a generous gulp of his tea.

"None whatsoever. It's not like we bring unused drugs home from the hospital. I can't imagine what the intruder was looking for!" Still mystified, she looked around the room as she slowly shook her head.

"Make any big purchases recently?" Boomer suggested. "I hear some people stalk the sidewalks on trash day, seeing who puts out a box for a big screen TV or new computer, that kind of thing."

Laurel motioned toward the modest-sized television in the room. "Neither big nor new," she said. "The one in the bedroom isn't much different. And both are still in place, along with my computer."

"Smaller electronics? New iPhone or iPad? Someone could have been in the store while you were and followed you home."

"It's time for an upgrade, but I've never gotten around to it."

"Hmm." He twirled his half-full glass as he seemed to give the matter more thought. "Bought any new jewelry lately?"

"I don't wear much. Working in the ER doesn't exactly call for diamonds."

He glanced at her bare fingers. "Had any rich relatives die lately? I saw a movie one time about a woman who inherited a fancy diamond necklace from an aunt she never even knew about. The lawyer who drew up the will was crooked and decided he wanted it for himself, so he broke into her house and stole it."

"No rich relatives that I'm aware of and no new deaths, thank goodness. I should be good on the inheritance theory."

"Hey, you never know," Boomer said, shrugging his shoulders. "I was just trying to think of reasons someone would break in and not taking anything." He drained his glass in a single gulp. As he set it down, a new thought occurred to him. "Any gifts? A bracelet or earrings? Have you checked all your hiding spots?"

A smile played on her lips. "What makes you think I have any hiding spots?"

"I thought all women had hiding spots. I know my sisters did. My mom, too. When she thought we weren't looking, she would slip a few dollars into a shoebox she kept in her closet."

"That may come in handy when you live among nosy family members, but I don't have to keep a secret hiding spot. It's just me here."

"Hey, I live alone, but even I have a hiding spot. You never know when someone could break in, like they did with you, and rob you blind. Everyone needs a secret hiding spot or two."

"I suppose so."

His green eyes twinkled. "Want to know where one of my favorite secret hiding spots is?"

"If you tell me, it won't exactly be a secret, will it?"

He remained undaunted. "Aw, we're friends. I don't have to worry about you stealing from me. Just like you don't have to worry about me stealing from you."

"True."

"I have two favorites, actually," he went on, even though she hadn't asked. She considered them more acquaintances than true and fast friends; certainly, nowhere near the sharing-secrets phase. "I have a cereal box in the top kitchen cabinet, where I keep a little extra cash, papers, that sort of thing. But my super-secret spot is—"

"Maybe I shouldn't hear this?" Laurel asked, covering her ears with an exaggerated gesture. She didn't want him mistaking this as some sort of bonding experience.

Boomer shot her a look that said '*really?*' but never veered from his subject.

"—inside a box marked 'poison.' It's for rats or gophers, or something like that. I figure who in their right mind would mess with a box that could possibly contain a death wish?"

Laurel looked skeptical. "Are you including yourself?"

He merely laughed off her comment. "Nah, it's a fake. Great place to hide small valuables. If you don't already have a spot like that, you may want to consider one. This time they may not have taken anything, but you may not be so lucky next time."

"I hope there *is* no next time!"

"You should still plan ahead," he insisted. "Unless you already have a hiding spot?"

His look was so pointed, Laurel felt obliged to answer. "Not—Not really," she confessed. "A fake drawer in my jewelry box is all, but it's so tiny, it doesn't hold much."

Boomer shook his head in silent reprimand, the censure clear in his eyes. "That's a terrible place. You know that, right? What would keep someone from taking the whole box with them?"

Laurel offered a meek wince. "They didn't take it this time, if that's any consolation."

"It's not. You really should find a more reliable spot." He held up a beefy finger to warn her before she said something foolish. "And don't you dare say the inside of the toilet tank. That's so overdone in the movies, it's the first place a burglar looks."

"And here I am, thinking how original my idea was." She spread her hands wide in mock defeat. "Guess I'll have to resort to a safe deposit box."

"You have one?" Boomer asked.

"Yes, but it's probably grown dusty and overgrown from neglect."

"I'll help you find a proper hiding spot, if you like," her co-worker offered.

"Thanks, but that won't be necessary." To herself, she thought, *Geesh. Obsessive, much?* Aloud, she offered a tea refill.

"I don't mind if I do. That's really good tea."

"Old family recipe," Laurel joked.

Boomer was roaming the living room again as she returned. He turned from straightening a watercolor painting on her wall. "It looked a little woppy-jawed," he explained. "I hear burglars even check the backs of artwork, thinking people could have something taped to the back."

"So, no taping treasures to the back of artwork," Laurel replied smartly. "Got it."

Taking a seat on the sofa again, he asked, "Did you think of anything I can help you do?"

"No, but I do appreciate the offer."

"I could house-sit for you while you go to the dentist."

"Dentist?"

"You said you had an appointment," he reminded her. "Remember? Yesterday, when I stopped by?"

"Oh. Oh, right. Uhm, I think that's tomorrow." She made a face. "To be honest, I haven't given it another thought." *Mostly because I made the whole thing up.*

"Still. I can stay here if it makes you feel better. You know. If you're uneasy about leaving so soon after the intrusion and all."

Hearing his offer, she felt doubly guilty for the lie. She tilted her dark curls to one side and offered a heartfelt smile. "That's really sweet of you, Boomer. But I'll probably just reschedule. I'm not sure I'm up to a dentist's drill after all this."

The blond man grunted. "I know that's right."

After a bit of small talk, Boomer finished his tea and stood. "If there's nothing I can help with, I guess I'll get out of your hair," he said. He sounded none too pleased with the prospect of leaving.

"Thanks for the offer, but I've—"

"Look at that mess on your floor!" he broke in. "Do you have a vacuum cleaner?"

"Yes, but—"

"I'll get that cleaned up and cleared out in no time. I'm good at laundry, too, if you need me to carry anything out to the clothesline."

"I hate asking you to help," Laurel protested.

"You didn't. I offered."

Despite the half-hour rest, she was still exhausted, and the laundry was only half-done. "If you're sure..."

"I am. Tell me where you keep your vacuum, and I'll do all the floors."

"I've already swept once, but I guess I missed some."

"Between us, we'll have it spic and span in no time," he promised with a big smile. "You don't by chance have an apron, do you?"

"An apron?"

"You know, one of those things you wear while cooking or working around the house. Little pocket here, a tie back there." He used his hands to demonstrate.

"I know what an apron is." She laughed, mentally picturing a frilly version on the big man. "I even have one, but it happens to be in the wash right now."

"Hope there was nothing valuable in the pockets." At her puzzled expression, he elaborated, "You know, like the family tea recipe, or something."

"Lucky for me, I keep that up here." She tapped the side of her temple.

"Good to know." Boomer rubbed his hands together in anticipation. "Now, if you'll introduce me to your vacuum, I'll get started."

While Laurel continued washing clothes and dusting every surface in her house, Boomer vacuumed and mopped the floors. He made the work look fun, doing silly dances and going to outrageous lengths in his quest to make the old house spotless. He even did the closet floors.

Boomer cheerfully hauled baskets of wet laundry outside and helped hang them before bringing the dried laundry in. The work went twice as fast with two sets of hands, and she found his upbeat sense of humor helped with the drudgery, as well as the depression.

When they were done, it felt only right offering to feed him.

"You're not cooking. Not after I hand-scrubbed that kitchen floor!" Boomer admonished.

"One, you used a mop. Two, who said anything about cooking? I was going to order in."

"Why don't we just go out and grab a bite to eat?"

"I'm hot and sweaty and hardly fit for a cleaning partner, much less the public." She fanned her flushed face, knowing her curls had kinked unmercifully with the day's labor.

"You look as gorgeous as ever, but I understand. I don't feel so daisy-fresh, myself." He made a show of checking beneath dampened arm pits, pretending to gag from the odor. "Just call me Pepe Le Pew."

"We'll hold our noses and gobble down our food," Laurel promised. "What's your favorite takeout?"

"Hard to beat a *Whataburger*," Boomer said with a grin.

"Do they deliver?"

"I'll be happy to pick them up and bring 'em back here."

"Only if you let me pay."

"That's not nec—"

She cut him off from further protest. "I insist. Just let me grab my purse." Her phone rang as she headed into the bedroom. Seeing Cami's number, she answered on the go. "Hey, Cam. You already off work?"

"No, but I will be soon," her friend said. "I wanted to know if I could bring a bite over before I come to help."

"Thanks, but that's not necessary. I think it's all been done. The last load of laundry is in the dryer now."

"Wow, you're fast! I was going to recruit Danni to come, too."

"I have to admit, I had help."

"Cade?"

"No. Boomer."

"Boomer?"

"Yeah, he's been a big help. Now if I can just figure out where I left my... oh, there it is." Spying her purse in an unusual location, she shook her head in wonder. The man had even vacuumed under her bed. She found her wallet and pulled out a twenty. "Hey, why don't you join us? He's making a *Whataburger* run." She pulled another ten out and tucked her purse away again.

"Nah, I don't want to intrude."

Laurel dropped her voice so that it didn't carry. "Please? I mean, like, *please*?" Without another word, she relayed to her friend the importance of having a third person present. She didn't want the man getting any ideas about today being a bonding experience.

"When you put it that way..."

Walking back into the living room, Laurel's voice brightened. "No, of course we don't mind! Do we, Boomer?"

"Mind what?" he asked in a clueless manner.

"This is Cami. She's headed this way and wanted to bring something to eat. I asked her to join us. You don't mind, right?"

To his credit, the disappointment went no further than his eyes. He pasted on a fake smile and said in a cheerful, booming voice that carried over the line, "As long as she keeps her hands off my ketchup, we're good. I know how she likes their fancy ketchup."

"He's right." Cami laughed. "I do. Hey, text me y'all's order, and I'll swing by on my way in. Save him the trip."

"Sounds good."

"I'm off in five. See you soon."

CHAPTER SEVEN

For a day that didn't bode well, the evening turned out better than expected. Boomer kept the jokes rolling and both women laughing. It helped quell the dark cloud still hanging over Laurel's heart and pushed back the shadows that lurked in every corner.

Even before Cami asked, she had already decided to spend another night in her friend's guest room.

"I'll wait for you to lock up," Boomer offered. "I'll even follow you ladies to make sure you get safely to Cami's."

Laurel shook her head. "Thanks, Boomer, but that's not necessary." He had been a huge help, but she hadn't intended to reveal her plans for the evening to him. He was in the room, however, when Cami asked, and there was no graceful way to exclude him from the conversation.

With a sincere smile, she all but pushed him out the door. "You've been a huge help today, but you're officially off duty now. You can go on. I just need to grab a few clothes, and Cami will follow me out. We'll be fine."

"I'm sure you will be," he agreed stubbornly. "But I'm not leaving until you do."

She huffed out a deep breath, his insistence beginning to perturb her. "Honestly. It's not necessary."

"Call it for my own peace of mind. I don't need to remind you that just one day ago, someone broke into your house. They didn't take anything then, but who knows if they plan to come back?"

"Gee, thanks, Boom!" Cami huffed, slapping the big guy's arm with the back of her hand. "We spend the entire evening bolstering her courage, assuring her there's nothing to be afraid of, and you blow it in three seconds. What is wrong with you?"

To his credit, Boomer hung his head in a show of regret. He looked chagrined. "I'm sorry. I didn't mean it the way it came out. It's just that... with the professor being killed at the hospital and all..."

Laurel's head snapped up. "Killed?" she asked, her tone cautious. To her knowledge, the specifics details of her death hadn't yet been released. The news channels were still indicating it was due to natural causes.

Boomer rubbed the back of his neck. "Yeah, well, that's what I heard." He hem-hawed around, avoiding direct eye contact. "I figured you already knew that, with your friend in the police department and all."

"Cade's working another case," she said, her tone frosty.

"I don't think it's official or anything, but I heard they're leaning toward ruling it a homicide."

Laurel avoided his direct gaze. She knew the true cause of death, as did Cami, but it was supposedly still under wraps. Logic told them it wouldn't stay that way for long, but neither wanted to be guilty of leaking confidential information. Fueling hospital gossip was just as bad.

"I hadn't heard that." Laurel was evasive. "I know she had a severe asthma attack. I witnessed it firsthand."

Boomer shrugged. "I'm just saying what I've heard. I thought it was weird, the police hanging around the way they did, asking so many questions. Now word is that they think she was killed."

"How?" Laurel asked, never hinting that she already knew the answer. "Suffocation? Something in her IV?"

"Not sure. But I hear we're all under suspicion. They think it could have been an inside job."

Laurel's stunned expression was real. The news was nothing new to her, but it still amazed her. She simply couldn't imagine a motive. "Why would anyone at *Texas General* want to kill a world literature professor?" she asked, not for the first time.

"Beats me, but that's the word in the halls," Boomer said. "So, forgive me if I'm being a little jumpy, but I just don't think any of us should take any chances right now. Safety in numbers and all that." He shivered for effect.

"Safety? What are you talking about?" Cami wanted to know.

"Hey, our girl here was the last person to see the prof alive," he pointed out. "Then her house gets broken into. If she saw anything..."

"I didn't," Laurel was quick to say.

"Maybe you did and just don't realize it. I saw a movie one time where—"

Laurel's patience had reached its limit. "You watch too many movies, Boomer. I'd rather not hear about the plot, thank you very much. And for the record, I think both of you are over-reacting." She pushed through her friends, heading into her bedroom.

Boomer looked at Cami with curiosity. "You've discussed this with her before?"

Not quite ready to confess any prior knowledge of the professor's murder, Cami tossed her palms up. "Hey. You can never be too cautious."

He studied her for a moment but eventually nodded his head. He was unusually solemn when he said, "I'm not sure I trust her cowboy to keep her safe. It may be up to you and me."

Cami twisted her mouth. "Meaning?"

"I think one of us should be with her at all times."

"Don't you think that's a little drastic?"

The tech rubbed his neck again, looking uncertain. Then he leaned forward and confided in a low voice. "Look. I didn't want to say anything earlier, but I thought I heard someone in the bushes outside earlier. I checked it out, thinking it might be a cat, but I didn't see anything. But I could have sworn I smelt a lingering hint of cigarette smoke."

Cami was now frightened. "That—That's scary," she said. "You really think someone is stalking her?"

"I don't know, but I don't want to find out too late that someone was. I think the best thing we can do is keep any eye on her. Make sure she's never alone."

"I doubt she'll go for it," Cami predicted.

"Then we'll just have to make pests of ourselves."

Cami gave her friend a few moments alone before knocking on her bedroom door.

"Laurel? You ready to go? We've got the kitchen cleaned and everything ready for lockdown."

"You can come in."

Cami pushed open the door, only to find Laurel seated on the bed. "All packed?" she asked brightly.

"I changed my mind. I'm not going with you tonight."

"I, uh, don't think that's a good idea. I thought we agreed you were coming back to my house tonight."

"And what about tomorrow night and the night after?"

Uninvited, Cami helped herself to a seat beside her friend. "You're welcome to stay for as long as you like. You know that."

"I appreciate it, Cami. I do. But I have to stay home at some point. It may as well be tonight."

After a quick knock, Boomer pushed his wide shoulders through the opened doorway. "Ready? I'll carry your bag out for you."

"She says she isn't going," Cami informed him. Over the back of Laurel's dark head, she gave him a what-do-we-do-now look.

"Huh? What's this?"

Laurel spoke for herself. "I appreciate what both of you are trying to do for me, but I've decided I can't allow this one incident to drive me from my home. At this point, I have no reason to believe this was anything more than a random break-in. The intruder didn't take anything, mostly because I don't have much of real value to take. I'll just have to put my big-girl panties on and go on like nothing has changed."

"That's all fine and good, Laurel," Cami agreed, "but don't you think it's too soon? Wait at least another day or so."

"I think that's a good idea," Boomer backed her up. "Go home with Cami tonight and give yourself time to make a decision with a clear head. You know how hard you worked today. You're probably too tired to think this through."

"All the more reason to stay home tonight. I'll be so exhausted, I'll sleep like a log, and I'll have the hardest night—the first one— behind me."

"Wouldn't you rather wait until your alarm is installed?" suggested her friend.

"You're getting an alarm?" Boomer sounded surprise. He bobbed his blond head in approval. "That's good. That's real good. When are they putting it in?"

"Monday. They were able to work me in on short notice."

Cami had an animated suggestion. "So, spend two more nights with me, and you'll come home to a safe, secure home. That way, we'll all have a more peaceful mind."

"I really think—"

Boomer didn't say anything, but he advanced into the room. He walked over to her window and pushed aside the curtain, peering into the darkness of the backyard. With his broad back blocking her view, Laurel couldn't see what he was doing.

"Did you open this window?" he asked her suddenly, turning back to face her.

"No. Why?"

"Because it's slightly ajar. I distinctly remember closing this window this afternoon."

"Are you sure?" Cami asked, hopping up to see it for herself.

"Maybe you just thought you closed it. It's an old house," Laurel pointed out. "Not everything is exactly straight, you know. Sometimes I have trouble getting the windows to latch."

"I'm pretty sure I did ..." he said, shaking his blond head in rebuttal.

"That settles it," Cami decided. "You're coming home with me tonight. I won't take no for an answer."

Backing her up, Boomer crossed his beefy arms over his chest. "I'll carry you out, if I have to."

Laurel huffed out a defeated sigh.

"Fine. You two win. I'm staying with Cami tonight."

Their gloat was cut short when her telephone rang. Seeing Cade's number on her screen, she motioned for them to give her a moment alone.

"We'll be waiting in the living room," Cami whispered, scooting past her with Boomer on her heels.

Laurel rolled her eyes, exasperation bleeding into her voice as she answered the phone with a sharp, "Hello?"

"That doesn't sound very welcoming," Cade's deep voice boomed. "Maybe I have the wrong number. I was looking for Lovely Laurel.'

"You've reached Lousy Mood Laurel," she said on a sullen whine.

"Uh-oh. Things really went south since we talked, huh?" He sounded sympathetic.

"You could say that."

And we didn't talk, she clarified, if only in her head. *We texted!*

"I can't say the same for me. About going south, that is."

"Really? You sound about as grumpy as I am."

"I was speaking geographically. I'm sitting at Love Field, waiting to catch a connecting flight to Phoenix."

"Phoenix? What for?"

"Hot tip on my murder investigation."

"Oh." Surprise was evident in her voice.

"I'm afraid I'll need another raincheck," he told her.

What else is new? Biting back the report, she instead said, "Sure. It looks like I'll be bunking with Cami again for a couple of nights, anyway."

"Why? Are you uncomfortable staying at the house? Is that the reason for the lousy mood?"

There was no need to bother him with the details, not when he would be hundreds of miles away. "Let's just say that things are still a mess."

"I'll sorry I'm not there to help. I caught this case at a bad time."

"Is there ever a good time for murder?" she countered.

"Never." Above the muffled sound of airport chatter and intercoms, he continued, "If everything goes well, I should be back by Monday."

"For your sake, I hope it goes well." Quite abruptly, she added, "Safe travels."

A tentative "Laurel?" kept her from hanging up.

"Yeah?"

"Are you sure everything's okay? You sound—"

"Like I'm in a lousy mood?" she supplied.

She knew she wasn't making it easy for him. She knew he was simply doing his job. She also knew a lousy mood was her best excuse for this irrational sense of betrayal she felt.

"I guess." He still sounded hesitant. After a beat, he asked, "Are you sure that's all it is?"

She gave a fraction of an inch. "Exhaustion may play a part in it, too."

Another muffled sound in the background, and rustling. "Look, they're calling my flight. Maybe I'll catch a break and be done sooner than expected. I still owe you dinner, you know."

Instead of acknowledging his elusive promise, she said, "Good luck with your case."

"Laurel, I—" Sensing her frostiness, Cade finished on a quiet, "I guess I'll let you go, then. For what it's worth, I'm glad you're staying with Cami. I won't worry about you so much this way."

"They hounded me until I finally relented," Laurel grumbled.

He half-chuckled at her complaining. "Tell the Curly Girls I appreciate their hounding."

He assumed Cami and Danni were behind the needling, and she didn't bother correcting him.

"Take care of yourself, Lovely Laurel. I'll see you soon."

"You be careful, too," she said.

Her mood hardly improved as she grabbed her bag, stalked to the door, and led the caravan to Cami's house.

CHAPTER EIGHT

It took some needling, but Cami convinced Laurel to join her for Sunday brunch. She insisted her friend needed all the comfort food she could get right now and knew just the place to take her. A small bed and breakfast just outside town was well-known for its extravagant country-style breakfast, and Danni was available to join them. What, she asked, could be better than comfort food with her two best friends?

Partly because she could think of no reason to object and partly because she was avoiding going home, Laurel agreed to join them.

Despite the good food and the good company, her mind kept straying back to the professor's death. "You were at work yesterday, Danni," Laurel said. "Have you heard any new gossip about Professor Tonchev's death?"

"There's always gossip, girlfriend. You know that." She grinned as she her slid her fork into the grits and cheese casserole and brought a bite to her mouth. Her eyes closed in sheer delight. "Oh. My.

Gosh! I think I've died and gone to Heaven. Have you tasted this?"

"I'm too busy obsessing over this tomato quiche," Cami replied.

Pushing the food around on her plate more than actually eating it, Laurel mumbled something about trying it on her next trip to the buffet.

Two more bites of the casserole dish, and Danni asked, "Why do you ask about the professor? Have you heard anything?"

"Boomer said word in the halls is that she was murdered. While *we* may know that's true," Laurel made a motion with her empty fork, encompassing the three of them, "I didn't think it was common knowledge yet."

"I haven't heard any specific gossip about it, but it wouldn't surprise me. These sorts of things are pretty hard to keep quiet."

"I wonder why the police haven't released a statement about it yet?" Cami wondered aloud. "I think they're still calling it an 'undetermined' death."

"My guess is they don't want to alert the killer," said Laurel.

With a wry tone, Cami turned to Danni, "Boomer was kind enough to remind us that we're all under suspicion."

Danni nodded her rust-colored curls. "It's weird, isn't it, thinking one of us might be a murderer?"

The thought was sobering. The three friends ate in silence for a moment, until Danni spoke again. "Oh. One thing I did discover is that the professor had a nickname. Her students called her Professor Top Chef."

Cami made a face. "That's sort of strange."

Almost choking on her bite of scrambled eggs, Laurel swallowed quickly and sputtered out a cough. "You know what's even stranger? Nurse Winslow called her the same thing!"

"How would he know that?" Danni asked.

"When?" Cami demanded. "When did he call her that?"

"Friday, when I literally ran into him at the grocery store. It was like a slip of the tongue. When I asked what he said, he quickly corrected himself and got all snitty with me. Two seconds later, he underwent a complete transformation and acted completely normal. And by normal," Laurel clarified, "I mean like you and me normal, not Trevor normal."

"He is an odd one, that's for certain," Danni said. "The guy's been on staff for three or four months now, and I still know nothing about him, other than he's divorced."

"Goes to show you how well I know him," Laurel mumbled. "I didn't even know that."

"All I know is that he went through a bitter divorce sometime within the past year. Believe me, once he gets started on the topic, it's hard to get him off it."

"Hmm. So, wonder how he knew the professor's nickname?" Cami asked. "Were they already acquainted?"

"Not that I'm aware of. He never mentioned it, at any rate," Laurel said.

"Then why do you have that look in your eye?" Danni accused.

"Because I just remembered something. Right after you left to get the security guard, Trevor came into the room. He said he was there to make the body presentable for her family, who was already on their way. But how did he know that? How did he even know she *had* a family?"

"It would be a safe assumption," Cami pointed out. "Most of us do have families."

"But the professor was from Bulgaria. I've since learned that she wasn't married and has a sister who lives in the Houston area, but I didn't know that at the time. So, how did Trevor know?"

"It could have been in her chart."

"I guess." Laurel set her fork down with a sigh. "Maybe I'm making too much of it. Maybe I'm allowing my personal opinion of the man to color my professional opinion of him. Like you reminded me, he's very good at his job and very thorough. I'm sure that's what he was doing that night, simply being thorough."

"I'm sure you're right." Cami nodded in agreement, setting her blond curls in motion. "What else could it be?"

"He's a good nurse," Danni reiterated. "He was simply doing his job."

Is it just me, Laurel wondered, or do we sound like we're trying to convince ourselves of that fact?

Her voice dubious, she still went through the motions of agreeing. "You're right, of course. He was just doing what any of us would have done."

With brunch over and nothing else to delay her, Laurel drove herself home. Her friends tried persuading her otherwise, but Laurel was determined to go back to her Craftsman.

She hated that she no longer felt safe in her own home. She went through each room, checking for signs of an intruder or anything out of place. When everything checked out, she finished folding clothes left in the dryer and returned all the newly laundered items to their rightful place.

She couldn't explain it, but Laurel had the oddest sensation that someone was looking over her shoulder. She even turned a couple of times, only to find nothing and no one behind her.

Logically, she knew no one was there, but it didn't keep her scalp from prickling and her skin from tingling. The slightest noise set her nerves on end. She resorted to turning the television on to fill the sound of silence. Just days ago, the silence had been her friend, offering a sense of serenity.

Now, it just seemed empty.

Worse yet was the way she second-guessed everything. Had that picture been slightly askew when she left? Was that curtain moved? In their frantic cleaning efforts yesterday, had she or Boomer left that drawer just slightly opened?

"Okay, you're being ridiculous!" she chided herself. "Enough is enough. No one has been here since you left last night. Nothing is out of place. Nothing is missing. You are simply a basketcase, and it has to stop."

She had one last load of laundry to do. She had re-worn the same pair of jeans yesterday as the day before. Knowing they were dirty and smudged with fingerprint dust, she could wash them with yesterday's cleaning rags.

Checking the pockets, she found a crumpled tissue and a cough drop wrapper in one pocket. In the other, she found the necklace she had discovered and promptly forgotten. Pulling the golden chain out again, she tried to recall having seen it before, but it looked as foreign to her now as it had when she first found it. The only new revelation she had was that the clasp was broken. She palmed the necklace in one hand, started the washing machine with the other, and then carried the chain with her into the bedroom.

She left it on the dresser and started out of the room, but something had her turning back. For no good reason, Laurel rethought her decision to leave the necklace lying out in the open. After a frustrating moment of indecision, she went with the less-than-original idea of putting it into her jewelry box's 'hidden' drawer. The box was a popular model sold nationwide, so the idea of a secret hiding spot was ludicrous. It was the best she could do, however, and it made her feel marginally better. Even though the necklace didn't appeal to her tastes, it looked valuable. She had no doubt the chunky chain was made of real gold, as was the medallion at its center. She recognized some of the Greek symbols on the coin-like disc and deduced the necklace had religious connotations.

"I need to turn this in to the hospital's lost and found," she reminded herself aloud. "Someone is probably frantic with worry. I'll put a note in my calendar for when I go back to work Tuesday."

It came as no real surprise, but she didn't hear from Cade that day. Logically, she understood his silence, but it didn't keep it from hurting. She knew he was in Phoenix on an important case, but a small part of her thought he might take a moment out of his day to send her a text. Anything, just to let her know he was thinking of her.

Her phone remained dark.

Less than two hours after their brunch, Danni called to insist she come early to Cami's. The two were making homemade lasagna for dinner and needed her help. Laurel suspected it was a ruse to keep her occupied and out of the house, but she appreciated the effort. She re-packed her bag and headed over to her friend's house for more Curly Girls therapy.

After dinner, they curled up in the living room for a relaxing evening. They started watching a television program, then abandoned it for conversation. Cami turned the set down low, rather than off.

A CASE OF STRANGULATION by A Stranger

When Laurel's phone rang, she had a moment of hope, thinking it might be Cade. Instead, an unknown number flashed across the screen.

"Oh, that could be Boomer," Cami said, noticing her frown. "Hope you don't mind, but I gave him your number."

Uncertain how she felt about it, she made no comment other than to answer his call.

When she hung up a few minutes later, Danni flashed a teasing grin. "Somebody has a crush," she remarked.

"He just got off work and was calling to make certain I was staying here again tonight," Laurel argued. "He was a big help yesterday, but too much like a mother hen."

"Because he likes you!" Cami pointed out, a twinkle in her eyes.

"The question is, do you like him?" Danni countered, swirling the wine in her glass.

"Everyone likes Boomer. He's just that kind of person."

"Don't be obtuse. Do you *like* him, like him?"

"What are we, in the fifth grade?" Laurel asked irritably. "He's a co-worker and casual friend. Period."

"The question is," Danni persisted, "would you be interested if Detective Hot Stuff weren't in the picture?"

Her answer came too swift and too sharp. "Detective Hot Stuff *isn't* in the picture!"

"Oh, no," Cami said, no longer teasing their friend. "What now?"

"Nothing. That's just the point. Absolutely nothing has happened, and I'm tired of sitting around, waiting for him to prove he's interested." Laurel turned her head away, as if to signal the subject was closed.

Less than a minute later, she whipped back around, her face filled with aggravation. "I get that he's out of town on a hot tip. I don't get that he can't take five seconds out of his day and send a text, even if it's nothing more than a silly smiley face."

"The day's not over yet," Danni said, trying to offer a positive spin on the subject. "Maybe he's still out chasing down suspects. It's an hour earlier in Phoenix, you know."

"He had to stop for coffee at some point," Laurel insisted. "A simple emoji isn't asking too much, is it?"

"You know how dedicated he is. Just like you are. If you're in the middle of a crisis with a patient, you aren't going to stop and send him some goofy smiley face, are you?" Cami argued.

"Whose side are you on, anyway?" Even Laurel could hear the whine in her words.

"Do you have to ask? You know—"

"Wait. Turn up the television," Danni broke in, pointing to the television. "It's a breaking news update. That's a picture of the professor!"

Cami turned up the volume so they could hear the story.

"The College Station Police Department has just announced that last week's death of Texas A&M University Professor Ylenia Tonchev has been ruled a homicide. Initially, the professor was admitted to the *Texas General Hospital* emergency department after a severe asthma attack. Doctors there treated her for the condition and reported she was responding favorably and was resting comfortably. Less than two hours later, she was found non-responsive in her recovery room. After extensive efforts to revive her, the professor was pronounced dead and it was generally assumed she succumbed to natural causes. This new allegation of murder has far-reaching and troubling effects, not only for her family and co-workers at the university, but for the hospital where she died. If you'll recall, last November, Dr. Arnold Fisk—"

"I knew it! I knew they would dredge all that up again!" Laurel cried. "They can't leave well enough alone. They have to remind us of every tiny blemish on the hospital's record."

"You know it," Danni snorted. "Wonder how Gaines is going to spin this one?"

Right on cue, the director of the hospital came on screen, expressing his deepest sorrow over the passing of the professor. He vowed to work tirelessly with the police department to find justice for the deceased woman and to make all resources available in their mutual quest for the truth. He came just short of denying that any of the *Texas General* staff was involved but stated that new protocols were already in place to 'fervently eliminate public access' to restricted areas.

"Nice way to insinuate someone outside the hospital is to blame for her death," Cami smirked.

"I don't know about you, but I certainly hope that's the case. I can't fathom the idea that we could be working alongside a murderer and not even know it." A shudder ran through Laurel's shoulders.

"I agree. It makes you wonder how well you really know your co-workers."

"Exactly."

With no other hard facts to report at the time, the news team showed a makeshift memorial at the university in the professor's honor. They interviewed a few of her students and former associates.

"That reminds me," Laurel said, only half-listening to the news now. "We work with her all the time, but did you two know that Dr. Ainsley is selling her house?"

"Seriously? Why?" Cami wanted to know.

"Said it was too big for just her and her husband."

"That's a shame. Her house is adorable."

Danni swirled her glass again. "Actually, I think I did know that. I overheard her talking about it one day. I don't remember who she was talking to, but it sounded like they were hoping to broker the deal for her."

With a roll of her eyes, Laurel muttered, "That would be Dawn Dyson, of Dawn Dyson Dreams Realty. She's her agent."

"No, it was a guy, but I can't remember exactly—Wait! Look at that." Danni pointed to the television screen again. "They're interviewing one of the professor's associates. Doesn't that say Marissa Winslow?"

"Yeah? What about it?"

"That's Trevor's ex-wife!"

"Turn it up."

An attractive woman with platinum-colored hair dabbed at her mascara-streaked eyes. "I—I just can't imagine it. Why would someone want to murder the professor? She was an excellent mentor, not only to me, but to all her students."

"You've been her TA for the past two years, isn't that correct?" the reporter asked.

Still sniffling, the woman nodded. "I'd like to think I was more to her than just a teacher's assistant. The professor and I had become close during that time. I went through a difficult time last year in my personal life, and she was always there for me, cheering me on and helping me fight my battles. I've been in shock since hearing of her death. And now to think that she was murdered..." Breaking down in true tears, Marissa Winslow turned away from the camera for a moment of privacy.

The Curly Girls watched in shock. Cami was the first to speak.

"Wow. So, Trevor *did* know the professor previously."

"At any rate, he had a direct connection to her," Danni agreed.

Laurel drew in an unsteady breath. "I—I don't like what I'm thinking," she admitted.

"What are you thinking?" Danni asked needlessly.

"The same thing you're thinking. That Trevor was resentful of the professor's friendship to, and possible influence over, his wife. He may have held her partially to blame for his marriage problems."

"Danni, you said how bitter he was about the divorce," Cami added. "I wouldn't put it past Trevor to hold a grudge."

"And he's just unstable enough," Laurel supplied, "to act on that grudge." She looked at her friend solemnly, her hazel eyes reflecting worry. "Seriously. I'm beginning to question the man's mental status."

"Are you saying what I think you're saying? That Trevor could have done this?"

"It makes sense, don't you think? He was there. He had access, and he had opportunity. And now we know he may have had motive."

"He did come back into the room," Danni mumbled.

"But why?" Cami challenged. "Why would he do that if he killed her?"

"To cover his tracks? Hide some sort of evidence?" Laurel suggested.

"Like what? Whoever killed her strangled her with his or her bare hands. You and I were there, Laurel," Danni reminded her friend. "We saw the bruising. There wasn't a lot of evidence to hide."

"Then we're missing something."

"Whoa there, missy. *We* aren't missing anything. This doesn't have anything to do with us. The police are handling this situation."

"How can you say it has nothing to do with us? With me? She was my patient, Danni! I failed her."

"You did no such thing!" her friends countered at once.

"You did everything in your power to make her better. You are not to blame," insisted Cami.

"She was responding, Laurel," Danni added. "I saw her charts. She was responding to treatment. Her death wasn't from any medical failings on your part. She was murdered, plain and simple."

Laurel disagreed.

"There's never anything simple," she argued, shaking her head, "about murder.".

CHAPTER NINE

"Laurel Danielle! How dare you keep this from me, your own mother!"

"I know. I'm sorry, Mom," Laurel apologized over the telephone. "I knew how excited you were about your class reunion. I wasn't going to ruin it for you before it even began."

"But your house was broken into! You shouldn't have to go through that alone. I should have been there for you," Angela Benson lamented.

"I haven't been alone, Mom. My friends have been very supportive. And I'm having an alarm system installed today. I'll rest easier once that's in."

"So will your father and I. But say the word, and we'll come straight home. We don't have to stay these extra few days."

"Nonsense. Stay and have a wonderful time. I promise to update you if anything else happens."

"Something else?" her mother asked, alarm evident in her voice.

"It won't," Laurel was quick to assure her. "I'm sure it was a random incident. Now tell me about your reunion. Did you have a great time?"

Twenty minutes later, Laurel hung up the phone, noting it was still minus any word from a certain handsome detective.

Another detective had called, however, and wanted to drop by the house to ask a few more questions. All routine, Detective Castilleja assured her when he made the request.

"I see you're having an alarm installed," he said upon arrival. The crews were all over the place, running wires and installing sensors. "Any particular reason to do that now?"

"Maybe you haven't heard, as you work homicide and not burglary. But someone broke into my house last Friday."

"The day after the professor's death?" he asked, eyes narrowing in surprise. Or perhaps in suspicion. Either way, the news took him unaware.

Laurel rubbed her forehead. "Was that only the next day?" She ran the sequence of events back through her mind. "Yeah, I guess maybe it was."

"What was taken?"

"That's the odd part. Nothing, as far as I can tell, was stolen."

Busy jotting down notes, the detective looked up. "Was the thief frightened away?"

"No idea. I ran to the store and while I was gone, someone broke in and ransacked my house. Made a huge mess of things but didn't seem to do any real damage."

"Do you have any idea what they may have been looking for?"

"Drugs would be my guess. For whatever reason, people seem to think nurses have access to drugs, which of course isn't true."

"You reported the break-in to the police, right?"

"Of course. They were the ones to suggest an alarm system."

"That's good. Very good."

"So, if you aren't here to tie the break-in to the professor's death, then I assume you have more questions about that night?"

"I do," the man acknowledged. He fixed his steady gaze upon her. "But why do you ask that? Why would I think the break-in had anything to do with the professor's death? Is that what you think, Miss Benson?"

Laurel felt like she was on the witness stand, being drilled by an overeager attorney.

"Honestly, I have no idea what to think," she told him. "I've lived here for three years and never had a moment's worry. Then, within a day of the professor's death, my home is broken into. My friends are worried it could be somehow tied together."

"I don't think I follow. Maybe you should spell it out for me."

"By all counts, I was the last person to see Professor Tonchev alive."

"Besides the killer, of course," he pointed out. The way he watched her made her nervous.

"Of—Of course. My friends think maybe I subconsciously saw something, or that the killer believes I may have seen something. What that could be, I have no idea. I've told you everything I can remember."

"Let's go over that one more time." He glanced down at his notes. "You say that the last time you spoke to the professor, she claimed to be cold and requested a blanket."

"That's correct. I took it as a positive sign, meaning the crisis had passed."

"And what crisis was that?"

"Her asthma attack, of course!" A bit exasperated, Laurel went back over the details with the detective. Again.

"We've been through all this," she said, when he circled back around to some of the questions for a third time.

"I realize that, Miss Benson, but sometimes witnesses recall things that slipped their mind during the first telling."

"But I've told you this almost a dozen times now. I left to get a blanket. Another patient called for help, and I assisted him back to bed. I stayed long enough to ensure he was stable. By the time I reached the professor's room, I—I was too late. She was already gone."

"And you're certain that the monitors were already unhooked when you reached the room."

"Positive!"

He nodded and let the topic go, but Laurel sensed it was only a temporary reprieve.

"Now, let's talk about what happened *after* the professor was pronounced dead. Can you walk me through that sequence of events?"

"Doctor Ainsley called the time of death, and we observed a moment of silence. I stayed behind after the last attendant left, trying to make peace with what had just happened."

"And why was that?" the detective asked, his eyes ever watchful.

"It's always difficult to lose a patient, but this one was especially hard. She was improving. The doctor and I were already discussing her release. By all rights, Ylenia Tonchev should have walked out the doors that night, not have been wheeled out on a coroner's table."

"I agree. But that's not what happened. And it's my job to find out what went wrong. So, tell me, again, what it was that made you call the doctor in for a closer evaluation."

"I noticed the bruising on her neck. Faint streaks of blue, in a circular fashion." She held her hand up to her throat as if to demonstrate a strangling motion.

"You were standing on her right, is that correct?"

"Yes. And I could clearly see the outline of fingers. I asked Nurse Barrington to confirm, which she did. We called the doctor back in, who also agreed with our assessment. We set up protocol on how to handle the situation, asked the security officer to make certain no one entered the room, and turned the matter over to the police."

"To your knowledge, did anyone come into the room after the three of you discovered the bruising?"

Laurel hesitated before answering honestly, "Another nurse started into the room, saw us inside, and left. I stayed until the security officer arrived. To my knowledge, no one else stepped foot inside."

"What nurse was this? The one who almost came inside?" he questioned.

"Nurse Trevor Winslow."

"And why was Nurse Winslow coming into the room?"

"You'll have to ask him that. I assume it was to make certain the body was presentable for her family."

Detective Castilleja asked several more questions, few of them new. He made Laurel uncomfortable, the way he watched her with shrewd and thoughtful eyes. She had the distinct impression he was hoping to catch her in a contradiction. After another fifteen minutes, he thanked her for her time and let himself out.

"If you think of anything else..."

"You'll be the first to know," she agreed frostily.

She didn't bother telling him about the weird sensation that she was being watched. She didn't mention the hang-up calls or the odd noises she thought she heard. She didn't utter a word about a crinkled curtain or a slightly opened drawer.

She didn't even tell him about the rug.

Yesterday, just before leaving for Cami's, she snagged her foot on the laundry room rug and left it askew. She started to turn back to straighten it, but she had her hands full and decided to let it go. When she came home this morning, the rug was neatly back in place.

No matter how many times Laurel tried to convince herself she simply didn't remember straightening it, she was 99.9% sure that wasn't the case. She had the distinct feeling someone had been inside her home again.

Not that Detective Castilleja would believe her. He didn't even believe her account of the night the professor died, and she had multiple witnesses and cameras to back up her claims. Why would this, a case of breaking and entering without theft, be any different?

For that same reason, she didn't tell the detective that Nurse Winslow had a previous connection to the professor. If he were as good a detective as Cade claimed, he would discover the connection for himself.

When the installer asked for her attention, Laurel gladly set aside thoughts of both detectives. She was much more interested in learning how to engage and disable the alarm panel and how to work the cameras aimed at her doors.

The camera came in handy later that afternoon when an unexpected visitor knocked at her door. She used the feature to get a sneak peek before answering.

Of all people to be on her doorstep, she never expected to see Dawn Dyson. Yet there the realtor was, dressed to perfection in a red skirt and jacket, with a briefcase at her side and a smile already plastered on her lips.

Curious, Laurel opened the door. "May I help you?"

"I'm not sure, but I hope so," Dawn answered with a mega-watt smile. "You may not remember me, but we met in the ER. Dawn Dyson." She extended her hand for a firm handshake.

"Yes, of course I remember. How is your ankle?" Laurel glanced down to see that it was still puffy and wrapped in an Ace bandage. "The one Dr. Ainsley advised you to stay off," she added pointedly.

"I can't very well make a living like that, now can I? But if you'd be so kind as to invite me in, I could at least rest it for a moment."

Now there's an original sales tactic, Laurel mused. Unable to imagine what the woman was up to, she opened the door wide and invited her in.

"Oh, what an adorable home you have!" Dawn gushed as she stepped inside. "I see it has the original hardwood floors and crown moulding. Absolutely stunning."

"Thank you. Please, have a seat. You can rest your ankle on the coffee table if you like," she offered.

"First, do you mind if I take a peek around? This place is just so adorable!" Without waiting for affirmation, Dawn wandered into the dining room and on into the kitchen. Laurel had little choice other than to trail behind.

"Two-bedroom, two-bath?" she quizzed.

"Uhm, yes."

Dawn made herself at home, inspecting the space as she kept up a running commentary half under her breath. "A small laundry room, I see. Excellent, excellent. Always a plus. Looks like a nice backyard beyond." She clasped her hands together in delight and looked at Laurel for confirmation. "The bedrooms are on the other side?"

"Yes, but I'm afraid I don't understand your curiosity."

"Professional habit, I'm afraid," she said, flashing another mega-watt smile. "I simply adore homes, particularly ones from this era! The craftsmanship is unparalleled to what you find in today's new builds. I'm afraid I simply can't help myself when it comes to real estate."

Laurel positioned herself in front of the hallway, hindering any further exploration of her home.

"I'm sorry, but my bedroom is a mess. And you really should get off that ankle. Let's have a seat."

While clearly displeased at being stopped from her explorations, Dawn did her best to accept the gentle rebuke with a modicum of grace. She settled on the sofa but stopped short of propping her foot up, despite Laurel's urging.

If she waited for an offer of refreshments, she was soon disappointed. Laurel dared not leave the room, lest the nosy realtor resume her snooping. An awkward moment lapsed, making it apparent that Laurel was foregoing the customary hospitality.

"I'm sure you're curious as to why I stopped by," Dawn said at last.

"Yes. Very."

"It came to my attention that your home was recently broken into and vandalized."

Confused as to where the conversation was headed, Laurel's forehead wrinkled as she corrected, "That's partially true. I wasn't exactly vandalized. But I hardly see—"

"I can't imagine how that must feel, knowing someone has violated the private sanctity of your home!" Dawn slapped a hand to her chest, but the gesture seemed overdone to Laurel.

"It is disheartening," she agreed.

"Disheartening? Why, it's downright horrendous! I don't think I could ever feel comfortable again, knowing someone had been inside my home and snooped around."

A smile itched on Laurel's lips. *Sort of like you're doing now?*

Suppressing the smile, Laurel gave the woman a curious look. "Again. I hardly see how my break-in inspired today's visit."

"I often find that once something such as this happens to them, homeowners simply can't stay in their homes. I know this is an unsettling time for you, but I just want you to know that if you should decide to sell—"

The ghost of Laurel's half-smile hardened into a thin line.

"I won't." Her answer was short and firm.

"Never say never," the pushy realtor chirped. "The housing market has gone up dramatically since you purchased this house." She dug into her briefcase and pulled out some papers. "I took the liberty of running a few comps and a rough estimate of the current market value of your home. I think you'll be quite surprised when you see the numbers."

The woman's audacity left Laurel speechless.

"I—I can't believe you did this," she finally managed.

"Oh, it was nothing." Mistaking the words as a compliment, Dawn batted them away with a motion of her hand. "This is what I do, putting people in touch with their dream homes. And while this house may have become a nightmare for you, I have at least two clients who already see this as their dream come true. Take a look at these numbers and tell me what you think."

"I think you should leave."

At the flat tone in Laurel's voice, Dawn's eyes shot to hers. "What—Whatever do you mean?"

"I don't know what possessed you to take such outrageous *liberties*, as you call them, but I see them as an invasion of my privacy. I have no intentions of selling my home, Ms. Dyson. Your intrusion into this matter is neither needed, nor wanted. I'm afraid I'm going to have to ask you to leave."

"Please, Miss Benson, hear me out. I know you're upset. And who wouldn't be, with their home being broken into and violated in such a manner? It has to be unsettling. Downright frightening. If I were you, I'm not certain I could ever sleep here again." She allowed a shudder to wiggle through her body, a tactic that probably worked well with her male clients.

Laurel stared at the woman with growing fury. She knew what Dawn Dyson was doing. She was playing on Laurel's fears and insecurities in an attempt to create a niche for herself. She thought if she planted the seeds of doubt, she might find the opening she needed to convince Laurel to sell. She already had potential buyers lined up.

It was as despicable as scoping out Professor Tonchev's house the moment her death was announced.

Laurel squeezed the papers in her hand, crinkling them unmercifully. She stood and stalked to the door, wrenching it open.

"Get out."

"B—B—But..."

"Leave, Ms. Dyson."

It wasn't a request. It was an order.

Laurel was so angry, she missed hearing the buzz on her phone. Cade had finally bothered to text.

Back on Texas soil! Call you soon.

CHAPTER TEN

Thirty minutes later, Laurel was still seething.

She was so mad, she forgot to check the camera the next time her doorbell rang.

"What is this, Grand Central Station?" she muttered as she jerked the door open.

She expected one or both of her besties. It was just like the Curly Girls to come over, especially after her ten-minute rant on a group call.

If not them, she considered the possibility it could be Boomer. Her self-appointed guardian kept calling or texting, making certain she was okay. Had she seen any suspicious activity around the house? Anything out of order? She had her alarm set, right?

It was neither her best friends nor Boomer. Monica Ainsley's visit was as unexpected and shocking as Dawn's had been.

"Dr. Ainsley!" The shock was evident in Laurel's voice. It took her a moment to remember her manners. "Please. Come in."

"I'm sorry to drop in unannounced like this..." the doctor started apologizing.

"Not at all. I could use a distraction right now. Would you like some coffee? Tea?"

"Water would be lovely."

"Lime?"

"Please."

"Have a seat, and I'll be right out."

"If you don't mind, I'll come with you. I'd love to see more of the house."

A bit odd, but okay.

She led the way into the kitchen, where Monica Ainsley admired the simple farmhouse style. "I know granite and stainless steel are all the rage these days," the doctor sighed, "but they often strike me as cold. This soapstone is much warmer and more pleasing to the palette. And I love that brick backsplash. Subway tiles are so overdone."

"It does seem most houses are nothing but cookie cutter molds these days," Laurel agreed. She prepared their water glasses and handed one to her guest.

"Table, or couch?"

"Table. I love your dining room, as well. Bright and airy."

"Thanks."

The doctor asked several questions about the house, the neighborhood, and how long Laurel had lived there. Laurel thought some of the questions were a bit pointed for casual conversation, but she remembered that Dr. Ainsley and her husband were thinking of selling their home. She was probably considering attributes she wanted in a new home.

In many ways, the conversation helped reinforce Laurel's love for the old Craftsman and made her focus on its many positives, rather than its recent negatives. The break-in, she reasoned, had little to do with the house itself, and more to do with the sorry state of affairs the world was in. These days, people were always looking for a soft target and an easy hit. The addition of her new alarm system addressed part of that issue.

At the first opportunity, Laurel turned the conversation to the death-turned-homicide ruling for the professor.

"I suppose the hospital is in turmoil now that the police have officially ruled Professor Tonchev's death as murder."

"It seemed rather chaotic while I was there," the doctor agreed. "I had a short shift and left early."

"I wondered about that," Laurel admitted, tapping at her watch to indicate the time. It was too early for a twelve-hour shift to be over. "Do you know if they have any leads?"

"If they do, they aren't sharing them with us."

"I know you had a staff meeting this morning. How is Director Gaines handling all this?"

"About as expected. Remain positive, focus on our patients, never resort to gossip, and deflect, deflect, deflect. He's walking a fine line between insisting our hallways are safe, while insinuating this was someone from the outside. We're implementing a one-visitor-per-patient rule in the

ER, and he's considering extending it to the entire hospital."

"I hate to see that happen. In the gravest of conditions, it's often the visitors who need the support of another family member more than the patient themselves do."

"That's true enough. But maybe this will be over soon, and things can go back to normal."

Laurel squeezed the last drop of flavor from her lime wedge and re-stirred her water. She tried to come up with the best way to pose her question. "I know your sons attended A&M. Did you have occasion to know the professor? Before she came in, I mean?"

"No, I don't believe we ever met."

"Did you see the news story on her last night?"

"Yes."

"I was surprised to hear that Trevor's ex-wife was her TA."

"Really? I didn't realize that."

"She was one of the ones they interviewed. Marissa Winslow."

"I never made the connection. Then again, I know very little about the man. As we discussed before, he's. . . odd."

"That he is. I also understand he's very bitter about his divorce. His ex indicated that she and the professor were good friends, and the professor helped her through a difficult time recently."

"Being odd—even being downright ornery and obnoxious—doesn't mean he's capable of murder."

"Of course not. But what if the director's theory about a visitor doesn't pan out? That would be a huge coincidence. Someone with a grudge against the professor just happens to be at the hospital the same time she comes in?"

"Whether it was another patient, a visitor, or one of our own, that appears to be the case," the doctor pointed out. "That person was on scene when the professor came in, period."

Laurel's sigh was deep and heavy. "A crime of convenience does seem to be the logical conclusion. A case of perfect timing for the killer." A new thought occurred to her. "That, or it could have been a theft."

"A theft?"

"That would make sense, too, wouldn't it? The professor may have had a lot of cash in her purse, or a diamond bracelet no one noticed missing. The killer could have crept in to take it, she awakened, and then he or she panicked. The only way to keep the professor quiet was to strangle her."

The doctor chuckled. "You either have a very good imagination, or your cowboy detective has been sharing tales with you."

"I prefer to call it an inquisitive mind," Laurel countered.

The doctor laughed along with her before squirming in her seat. "Would you mind directing

me to the little girl's room? My bladder's not what it once was."

"Sure. First door on the left down the hall."

"Thanks. And thanks for the water, but that's all for me."

While the doctor was gone, Laurel cleaned up the kitchen. When her guest wasn't back after the glasses were washed and put away, Laurel wandered into the living room to wait for her.

"I confess," Monica said upon returning. "I peeked into the bedrooms. Your home is charming."

"Thank you." It sounded so much nicer, and more sincere, coming from her friend than from the presumptuous realtor.

"Would you object if I brought Robert by?"

"Robert? You mean, your husband Robert?" Hoping she didn't come off as rude, Laurel fumbled the recovery. "What am I saying? Of course, your husband. I mean . . . certainly. Of course he's welcome to come. Both of you are welcome to drop by anytime. Anytime, at all."

"I'd like his input before I get too carried away. The house is the perfect size for us and just as cute as a button." Monica looked around again, pleased with what she saw.

"Yes, you mentioned downsizing."

"I thought I wanted to be in a different neighborhood altogether, but Dawn convinced me to give this one some thought. I'm so glad she did."

An uneasy suspicion wormed into Laurel's thoughts. "Dawn? Dawn Dyson?"

"Yes, that's right. My realtor. Although I've considered giving someone else a shot at it. He's new in the business and just getting started." Her mind drifted off subject before something occurred to her. The doctor's eyes widened as she had a disturbing thought. "Dawn did stop by, didn't she? Please tell me you were expecting me, and I didn't just pop in out of the blue."

"She—She did stop in, but I'm afraid there's been some misunderstanding. My home is not for sale."

"Oh. Oh, my." Monica was clearly horrified at her blunder. She put both hands over her mouth and cried, "Oh, Laurel, please forgive me! I'm so embarrassed! I had no idea."

"There's nothing to forgive," she said easily, although inside, she was seething. Just like that, her ire at the real estate agent was renewed. "And I enjoyed our visit, so no harm done."

"Again, I'm so embarrassed! I never meant to barge in here and intrude on you."

"There's nothing to apologize for. It's fine. Really."

"Now that I have my foot out of my mouth, I do believe I'll be on my way."

Both women made light of the blunder, but it was a ruse on both their parts.

As Monica Ainsley hurried out to her car, Laurel saw a rare show of anger by the normally calm physician. Even from inside the house, she could hear a few of the hurled insults issued by one very embarrassed and irate doctor as she spoke to the realtor.

And even though she couldn't hear the exact conversation, she knew she couldn't agree more.

In a day filled with surprise guests, there were still two more in store for the evening.

Laurel declined Cami's invitation to stay another night, touting the security of her new alarm system. Not only was it time she face her fears and stay at home, but she knew she wasn't fit for decent company. Dawn Dyson's underhanded scheme still fueled a bad mood.

When Boomer showed up at her front door, she tried warning him. She wasn't in the frame of mind to entertain.

"What happened? Did someone try to break in again?" he asked in concern.

"Not exactly. But I did have an intruder."

"Who? Where are they? Do I need to handle this?" Despite her claims of wanting to be alone, he pushed himself through the front door, ready to go to battle for her.

"No. She's long gone by now."

"She? The intruder was a woman?"

"Yes. One very sneaky, pushy, presumptuous woman. Dawn Dyson!" She threw up her hands in outrage as if the name said everything.

"What was a real estate agent doing here?" he asked, looking somewhat alarmed. "You aren't moving, are you?"

"No! No, of course not. I love this house."

"You should. It's a great house." Not for the first time, he looked around with true appreciation. "I dabble a little in real estate, you know. This is a fine example of craftsmanship in the first half of the 1900s."

"You're into real estate?" For some reason, his statement took her by surprise.

"I'm not just an orderly, Laurel," he said, his voice taking on an edge. "I have more aspirations than just pushing around hospital beds and equipment for the rest of my life."

"I'm sure you do. I didn't mean to imply otherwise. I simply didn't know you were interested in real estate. Buying or selling?"

He shrugged his beefy shoulders. "A little of both. And I'm telling you. You have a gold mine in this little house. Don't let the likes of Dawn Dyson get to you, if you ever do decide to sell. Call me first. I can advise you."

"I don't intend to sell," she assured him. "Doesn't matter if she tries to push me, pull me, scare me, or bully me. It won't work."

"What happened?"

Laurel told him everything that had transpired, from Dawn's audacity to Monica's embarrassment. Simply talking about it got her all worked up again.

"Does the woman sit by a police scanner and wait for the next catastrophe to happen, so she exploits it to her advantage?" Laurel paced the floor in aggravation.

"Why do you say that?"

"Were you there when she came into the ER with a sprained ankle?"

"I don't think so. What happened?"

"It was the day after Ylenia Tonchev died. The woman had the audacity to go to the dead woman's house and snoop around! I know she was snooping because it was in the dark, and she admitted as much. She was all excited about showing the house to Dr. Ainsley."

"Say what?"

"I know! Can you imagine? It served her right, falling in the dark and getting all scraped up, not to mention spraining her ankle. She had no business being out there in the first place."

"I'm surprised she wasn't arrested for trespassing. That's a pretty swanky neighborhood. Highly sought after. Listings there don't last long."

"That was her 'excuse' for being out there. She wanted to get a jump on the market. How does she even know the family will sell the place?"

"Pretty safe bet," Boomer reasoned. "The sister has a home and a career in Houston. No reason to have a hefty mortgage in two places, no matter how well off she may be."

Laurel frowned. "Now you're sounding as analytical and calculating as Dawn," she accused. She truly was in a lousy mood.

"Hey, I'm just sayin'."

Laurel pinched the bridge of her nose and took a deep breath. "You know what, Boomer? It's been a really long day. I appreciate you stopping by to check on me, but I think what I need is a long, soaking bath and an early night in bed."

"I get that," he said agreeably. "But do you mind if I wash my hand off first? I have something sticky on the side of it here." He held it up for inspection, but she saw nothing, primarily because she wasn't looking that closely. She was beyond tired and ready for some peace and quiet.

"Yeah, sure," she said, waving him down the hall. "You know the way."

The doorbell rang again, and Laurel's head dropped back on her shoulders. "You *have* to be kidding me!" she muttered. She jerked open the door and stared at her latest guest in utter surprise.

Cade stood on the doorstep, looking as devastatingly handsome and rugged as ever. Perhaps even more so now, his jaw scruffy with stubble and fine lines of fatigue fanning out from his eyes.

"C—Cade. What are you doing here? When— When did you get back?"

"Just now. Didn't you get my text?"

"No, I guess not." After obsessing over her phone for the better part of two days, waiting on a single word from him, today had been so hectic, she hadn't even thought to check.

"Are you going to invite me in, or do I have to stand out here at night?" A devilish smile peeled back the corners of his mouth.

"Of course. Please, come in."

Cade stepped inside the house just as Boomer stepped from the hall.

"Hey, I went ahead and started your bath for you," the blond giant said, looking down as he wiped his wet hands on his jeans. "I think you're right. It's just what you—" He pulled up short when he saw the cowboy in the doorway. "Oh. I didn't know someone was here."

Cade inspected the man coming from her bedroom. Testosterone raged through the room as he sized up the man who was taller and heavier than he, but not nearly as fit and agile. If it came down to a battle of sheer strength, it was difficult to know who would come out the victor.

Beside her, Cade coiled as tightly as a clock. His voice sounded like one, ticking off the words, "I could say the same."

Can it get any more awkward than this?

Her head already pounding, Laurel lamely made the introductions. "Cade, this is a friend from work. Boomer, this is Cade."

"How ya doin'?" Boomer said, strolling over to offer his hand in casual greeting. "You're the cop, right?" He stood with his legs slightly apart, his bulky form positioned to form a barrier between Cade and the rest of the room.

"Detective," Cade corrected, taking his hand in a firm and aggressive grip. "And you are?"

"An associate of Laurel's at *Texas General.*"

It was a vague description, meant to imply they had a connection the lawman wasn't privy to. She didn't like the inference any more than she liked the way he stood there, acting as if he had more right to be in her living room than Cade. Still,

Boomer had been a good friend to her over the past few days.

And he's been here for me when Cade wasn't, she reminded herself.

She didn't want either man getting the wrong idea.

"There's been a lot going on the last couple of days, Cade. Boomer has been a huge help to me," she said, her smile sincere. "If it weren't for him and the Curly Girls, my house and I would still be a disaster."

"Speaking of disaster, maybe I should go turn off that bath water," Boomer offered.

"No!" She spoke more sharply than intended, but she didn't relish the thought of Boomer going into her bedroom again. Just knowing he had gone in there in the first place seemed overly familiar, even if his intentions had been innocent.

In a more moderate voice, she cleared her throat and said, "I mean, no, that's not necessary. Thank you, though. I'll take care of it."

Another awkward moment ticked by.

"So, I guess we should both go and let you take that bath." Cade's authoritative voice boomed in the thick air.

"Probably," she agreed.

Despite her encouragement, it was like an old-fashioned standoff. Neither man wanted to be the first to leave.

"My bath water..." she reminded them, prompting them both to turn reluctantly for the door.

Not the least bit intimidated by the other man's size, Cade made a motion with his hand, inviting Boomer to go first.

Boomer took it in stride. "Nice to meet you, copper."

A nerve ticked in Cade's clenched jaw, but his reply was cordial. "Same to you, associate." He never met Laurel's eyes as he turned to follow Boomer out.

Both men started down the walk, but Laurel couldn't let Cade leave like that, believing the worst. He had just gotten home and come straight here. Didn't that account for something?

"Cade."

He stopped, but he didn't turn around. Not until she said, "Please. Don't go.

CHAPTER ELEVEN

Cade held her eyes as he walked back to the house. In her peripheral vision, she saw Boomer climb into his big truck and roar off into the night.

Now that Cade stood in front of her, Laurel had no idea what to say. They were still where they were two days ago, caught between their careers and unsaid words. The ominous connotations of 'we need to clear the air' still echoed in her heart.

"I have to turn off the water," Laurel said, stalling for time. She fled before he could reply.

When she returned, he was on the phone, his profile to her. Old habits died hard as she read the situation before her.

Tight lines around his mouth. Stiff set of the shoulders and jawline. Feet braced for confrontation. Nostrils slightly flared, indicating bad news on the other end of the line. Taking a deep breath, fortifying himself for a fight. Laurel swallowed hard, her observation taking on a few personal notes. Or maybe it's to remind me of that lean, muscled chest. Of how much I've missed that smile that manages to break through the hard lines and reflect in his eyes. Of...

"Yes, sir," Cade said into the phone. "I understand, sir." He used his most formal voice, the one reserved for his duties as a police officer.

Laurel slipped up beside him as he ended the call. "You have to go, don't you?" she asked softly.

"Laurel, I'm sorry. I should have never come over here tonight."

"It wasn't what you think."

That smile she had missed softened the hard lines of his mouth. "Not that." He ran his hand over his stumbled jaw. "But it's late. We're both exhausted. And now my day just got longer."

"I'm sorry," she said softly, reaching up to rub a comforting hand along his upper arm.

His voice was ruefully raw. "Not as sorry as I am."

"You'll call me when you can?"

"I'm off tomorrow. If my boss says otherwise, I'll take a sick day. We have a long overdue talk, Lovely Laurel."

It couldn't all be bad news, could it, with that look in his eyes? With him calling her Lovely Laurel?

"I—I have to work," she said in dismay. Seeing the determined light in his eyes, she quickly added, "Come around seven thirty."

"I'll be here. And I'll bring those chicken fingers and wine that I owe you." With one arm, he pulled her to his side and dropped a kiss onto her forehead.

It wasn't the two-armed, mind-blowing kiss she craved, but this was easier to pull away from.

"Your bath water is getting cold," he said in a husky voice. "Set that fancy new alarm when I'm gone."

"How did you—?"

The look in his eyes warmed her even more than his words did. "You may not have thought so these past few days, but I'm always watching out for you, Laurel. I'm always worried about your safety."

The note in Laurel's phone reminded her to take the necklace with her for the hospital's lost and found. But when she opened the not-so-secret compartment the next morning, the golden necklace was no longer there.

"What? How could this be? I know I put it there!" she cried aloud.

Laurel didn't have much time to search elsewhere, but she knew her efforts would be fruitless. She was positive she had put the necklace in the box.

Driving in to work, she tried piecing the timeline together in her head. She had re-discovered the jewelry on Sunday, the day before her alarm system was installed. The same day she was certain the rug had been moved at her back door. Had someone been inside the house again?

"Don't panic," she told herself. "There has to be another explanation." Her mind came up blank, except for the obvious. "The only other explanation is that someone took it while I was home, alarm or not. So, who was at the house after that? Think, Laurel. That was only yesterday."

It felt more like a week ago, but she reassembled the previous day's events in her head. "Okay, who was there? All the men from the alarm company. The good detective Herschel Castilleja. Dawn Dyson. Monica. Boomer. Cade." She ticked them all off on her fingers, dismissing them as soon as they came to mind. "Okay, so I can't vouch for any of the alarm guys, but I doubt the necklace was worth losing their job over. I also wouldn't put anything past Dawn Dyson, but outright stealing doesn't seem her style. She much prefers to create more challenging opportunities. So, that leaves me with the conclusion that someone did in fact break into my house for the second time." The thought gave her the willies. "Thank God I have an alarm system now."

As expected, tension was thick when she arrived at the hospital. Suspicion floated in the air, fueled by gossip and short tempers. It was one thing when *she* knew a killer could walk among them. It was quite another when the entire staff was aware of it and were now eying co-workers with scrutiny and doubt.

"I hate this," Danni hissed, watching a group of aides whispering in the hallway. "How can we work in this atmosphere? Everyone is suspicious of the next person. There's no sense of trust."

"This is something new for us all. I'm sure it will pass soon enough." Not even Laurel believed the words. But hearing them, even from her own lips, somehow helped.

"Did you happen to notice the daggers flying from Trevor's eyes?"

"How could I not? I think one nicked me, they were so sharp. What's with him?"

"It hasn't escaped notice that his ex-wife was the professor's TA. Rumors are floating around that the two women were more than just friends, and he killed the prof out of jealousy."

Though spoken in low tones, fellow nurse Shanae Burns overheard them and put in her two cents. "The version I heard said he and the professor had a brief affair, she blabbed to the wife to break up their marriage, and he killed her for revenge. One thing is for sure. With that odd duck, anything is possible."

Shanae gave them a 'you know I'm right' look as she waddled into the hall. "Hey. Where's our man Boomer today? I thought he was on the schedule."

"Someone said he called in. Car trouble," Laurel answered.

It was cowardly of her, but she was secretly relieved he wasn't there today. She hadn't meant to hurt him last night, asking Cade to stay in front of him, but she told herself it was better this way. She had never intentionally misled him. He needed to understand there was no chance of a future between them. Not when her heart was already taken.

Thoughts of tonight's date filled her with equal parts fear and anticipation. She was half-afraid Cade might do the same thing she did with Boomer: set boundaries on their relationship, signaling that it went no further than friendship. The other half of her clung to hope, recalling the warm look in his eyes and the fact he was bringing wine tonight.

Breakups call for hard liquor, don't they? She reasoned.

Her friend broke into her daydreaming.

"Just so you know," Danni continued, speaking so low no one else could overhear. "I hear Trevor's gunning for you."

"Me?"

"Apparently, Detective Castilleja paid him a visit." Before she could say more, the wail of an ambulance broke up their conversation.

Laurel's lunch break came well after the noon hour. She took it in the hospital's cafeteria, needing a few moments away from the watchful eyes of her co-workers. Everyone knew she was the last person to see the professor alive, and the first one to discover her death. Gossip and unfounded rumors filled the gap in between.

Her peaceful break was interrupted by one very irate Trevor Winslow.

"Way to sell a co-worker out, Benson," he spat. Without invitation, he plucked out a chair from the table, spun it around, and straddled its back.

Laurel assumed the pose was meant to look manly and threatening.

"I have no idea what you're referring to," she said smoothly. Her tone turned sarcastic. "And please. Have a seat. Don't mind the fact I'm on my break."

"You know what I'm talking about. You told the police I tried sneaking in the room after the professor died."

"I did no such thing. I told them you came into the room, which you did. I never said nor implied you were sneaking."

"You told them I had no right to be in there."

"Not so. I told them to ask *you* why you were in there. Which poses an excellent question. Why were you there, Trevor?"

"I told you why that night. I was making certain the body was presentable for viewing. I knew her sister was on her way."

She crossed her arms and glared at him. "You never mentioned that you knew the professor prior to her ER visit."

"Why should I? She wasn't even my patient." He was right, but Laurel didn't appreciate the hateful tone in his voice.

"And thanks to Marissa's play for attention," he continued, "now everyone thinks I had something to do with the professor's death. Your implications only made matters worse."

"I didn't make any implications," Laurel insisted. "And this isn't all about you. They're talking about me, too, you know."

Trevor ignored her. "Gaines wants to speak with me this afternoon. If I get fired, this is all on *you!*" he spat.

"You could be arrested for murder, and you're only worried about your job?"

"I have nothing to fear. I have an impeccable record that speaks for itself."

Laurel noted that he said nothing about being innocent. Was he so arrogant that he thought it didn't matter? That his reputation alone was enough to carry him?

Yes, she realized. He was that arrogant.

"I don't know why they're looking at me, anyway," he sniffed. "I told the police they should be looking into the doctor."

"The doctor? You mean Dr. Ainsley?"

"Of course. She had more motive to kill the professor than any of us."

Totally dumbfounded, Laurel asked, "What are you talking about?"

"She wanted the professor's house. Marissa used to talk about it, saying how she kept badgering the professor to sell. She sent random gifts and notes, trying to soften Top Chef up. I even heard her on the telephone, telling her agent she would do *anything* to get her hands on that house."

Laurel was incredulous. "It was an expression of speech. I'm sure by 'anything' she didn't mean *murder!*"

"Oh? Are you really so sure?" he asked, arching his brows in a haughty manner. "Have you never seen the woman angry?"

She started to say no, but then she recalled the rant she overheard after Dawn sent the doctor to her house on a wild goose chase. At the time, fueled by her own anger, she thought the tirade was justified. But viewed in this new context, did it seem a bit excessive? Laurel had heard enough to know the doctor used some very harsh words. And the tone had certainly been bitter. Borderline threatening.

Here I go, no better than the rest of the gossip mongers! Laurel chided herself. Suspecting the doctor when I have nothing to go on but speculation and hearsay. And from Trevor, no less! The man isn't stable. First, he lashes out at me, now at Monica. He'll point fingers at anyone to take the pressure off himself.

"Being angry and being capable of murder are two separate things," she said instead.

Trevor abruptly stood from the chair, not caring that he pushed it over in his haste. He glared down at her, the anger evident in his own eyes.

"Not always," he proclaimed.

His tone was so flat and so deadly calm, Laurel couldn't help but believe it somehow held a threat.

CHAPTER TWELVE

Laurel hurried home from work and showered. She changed outfits five times before deciding on a semi-casual, cold-shoulder linen blouse in muted blue. Paired with white cropped pants and low-heeled sandals, she looked fresh and springy. And short.

Too short, she decided. She would have changed a sixth time, but the doorbell rang before she made it back to her closet.

She was a bit breathless as she opened the door.

Cade looked as handsome as ever in his worn, starched jeans and a western checkered shirt in dark blue. As usual, scuffed boots (minus the spurs), his oversized PRCA Championship belt buckle, and a straw cowboy hat completed his authentic cowboy persona.

"Hey," she managed.

"Hey, yourself," he replied, his eyes sliding over her with appreciation. He belatedly looked down at his rugged apparel and the sack of takeout he carried. "This is all wrong, isn't it? You look like filet mignon, and here I am with chicken fingers."

She laughed nervously. "This old thing? The important thing is you brought chicken fingers." She grabbed his arm and practically dragged him inside the house.

"Oo-kay, then," he said, narrowly missing the door as it shut behind him.

"Do you want to eat at the bar, the table, on the couch, or on the patio?" She rattled off the options at record speed.

"Laurel."

He said it in a way that made her look at him.

"What's going on? Why are you so nervous?" he asked, his voice softening.

She didn't quite meet his eyes. "It's been a long week. And a tough day back at work."

"Look, if you want me to go—"

Her answer came swiftly. "I don't."

A smile crinkled the corners of his brown eyes. "Good. Because smelling these all the way over has made me very hungry."

He didn't bother taking the bag into the kitchen. He opened it right there on the coffee table, settling the debate on where they would eat. Laurel hurried into the kitchen and loaded a tray with salad and other necessities. When she returned, Cade already had the wine uncorked and the chicken opened.

"This looks like a feast."

"Don't let my mother hear you say that. She'll punish you with massive amounts of food in what she deems a 'proper feast.'"

"Same with my mom," Laurel said, adding two of the meat strips to her salad.

"Speaking of your mom," Cade said causally, pouring wine into their glasses, "now that I impersonated her and all last week, don't you think I should actually meet the woman?"

Laurel froze in place, her mouth opened, and the fork poised in mid-air. Her eyes widened. "You *want* to meet my mother?"

Maybe he's not here to break up. Maybe there's hope for us yet.

He shrugged a broad shoulder. "Isn't that what usually happens? I show you my crazy relatives, you show me yours. That way we both know what we're dealing with?"

She eyed him suspiciously. "Who said I had crazy relatives?"

"All of us have crazy relatives. That's what families are all about."

"True."

"So?" he prodded.

"So, what?"

"So, when do I get to meet your parents?"

"Yeah, I don't know about that," Laurel said, more than a little flustered. "My dad can be a bit overprotective at times."

"Even if I assure him I have honorable intentions?"

"Even then. According to him, he was young once, too."

Cade grunted. "I think I passed young eight or ten years ago."

"You're an old man of … what? Thirty-one?"

"Two, in just a couple of weeks." He picked up his own glass. "By the way, my mother says to tell you you're invited to my birthday party. The entire family will be there, just so you know. Which means there's still time to take that cruise around the world if you're so inclined."

Her heart fell. *He's laying down the boundaries. Definitely just friends. His mom invited me.*

She drew in a shaky breath. "Tell your mom I appreciate the invitation, but—"

"Please?" he asked, his brown eyes beseeching hers. "I want you there with me."

Laurel's heart thudded crazily against her chest. "O—Okay."

Cade tipped his glass to hers. "To birthdays and crazy families."

They ate for a few moments in companionable silence.

"I take it you didn't have to call in sick?" she asked.

"I mostly worked from home. But I stressed the fact that I had plans this evening and wasn't to be disturbed."

"How's that case coming? Did going to Phoenix pay off?"

"Yeah, it did. We've got enough to make a solid arrest, but we want it to stick. Just tying up a few loose threads."

"And the professor's case? Have you heard anything new on that?"

"Still in the dark. I only know that they did clarify it was murder and are actively pursuing some 'promising leads.'"

"The hospital was abuzz with theories today."

Cade grunted. "I just bet it was."

"Trevor is convinced I sold him out and sicced the police on him."

"Trevor?"

"Oh, that's right," Laurel remembered, waving her chicken tender in the air. "You've probably never heard me complain about him. He's only been with us for a couple of months."

He arched a suspicious brow. "Is that your way of pointing out that I haven't been around much during that time?"

"No." Laurel frowned. "I mean, it's the truth, but that's not why I said it. Trevor Winslow has been a thorn in my side since he joined the nursing staff. He's one of those chauvinistic males who thinks it's beneath his station in life to have a female outrank him. He's rude, arrogant, borderline psychotic, and a pompous jerk."

"Then why did the hospital hire him?"

Laurel sighed. "Because despite his personality, he's also a very good nurse."

"So why does he think you sold him out to the police?"

"Detective Castilleja came by again yesterday to ask the same old questions for the twenty-third time. He finally threw in a new one. Had anyone come into the room after we discovered the bruising but before the security officer arrived? I told him yes. Trevor."

She saw the gears turning in his mind. "Why would he have been in her room?"

"He said he was making certain the body was presentable for the family. As it turns out, he had a prior connection to the professor. For all I know, he may have even known her sister and went the extra mile out of genuine concern."

"Did you mention that prior connection to Chel?"

"No."

"And why is that?"

Laurel shrugged, her tiny smile ever so smug. "You said he was a good detective. So I let him detect."

"You aren't giving him a hard time, are you? It's important that you cooperate with the investigation, Laurel."

"I know that. And I am cooperating. But he clearly doesn't believe me. That's why I didn't even bother telling him about all the suspicious activity around here."

Cade was instantly alert. "What suspicious activity?"

Oops.

"Uhm, nothing, really." She waved her hand vaguely through the air. "Just a few odd happenings after the break-in."

"What kind of odd happenings? And why didn't you tell me about them?"

"You were busy with your case. And then you were on your way to Phoenix, and there was nothing you could do, so. . ."

"So, you just didn't tell me? You kept it from me?" He sounded disproportionately angry at her admission.

"You were in Phoenix!" she threw back at him.

"I had to go, Laurel. I didn't have a choice."

"I know that. Just like I didn't have a choice about being harassed."

"Harassed? By whom?"

"I don't know. They didn't identify themselves when they called a half-dozen times. Or when they peeked in through the bushes. Or when they broke back into my house on Sunday night."

"What?" He stood so quickly, he almost upset the box of chicken. "You were broken into a second time? Why didn't you tell me?"

"Because I just realized it today."

"You're not making a lot of sense," Cade growled.

"Sit back down, and I'll explain." She tugged on his arm, forcing him to take a seat again.

She told him about finding the necklace and tucking it into her pocket before the first break-in. She explained that with so much else happening, she never gave it a second thought until she re-found it on Sunday.

"But when I went to get it this morning, it wasn't there. I'm positive I put it in the jewelry box because I thought of the convoluted conversation Boomer and I had about secret hiding spots. Yesterday was like a revolving door around here, but I'm fairly certain none of those people would have taken it. And then I remembered the rug, and I realized I must have been broken into a second time."

"What rug, and what people?"

After hearing the details, he looked surprised by the name of one of her guests. "Dawn Dyson? The real estate agent? Why was she here?"

"Long, sordid story, but that's the one."

"You know she was attacked last night and is in the hospital, right?"

"What?" It was Laurel's turn to jump from the couch in surprise.

"I don't have all the details, but someone broke into her house in the middle of the night and beat her within an inch of her life. She's in critical condition at *Brazos Valley Methodist.*"

Laurel was stunned. "I—I had no idea." She put her hand over her hand, holding in the cry of dismay threatening to leak out. A dozen random thoughts raced through her head.

I was so angry with her, but I never wished this upon her!

Monica Ainsley was angry with her, too. She all but threatened her. Could Trevor have been right? Could she have done this?

What if it had been the 'other' agent Monica was rumored to be using? Could this be about earning a commission? A way to eliminate the competition?

"Hey, now," Cade said, seeing the conflict in her face. "Whatever it is you're thinking, just stop. This doesn't have anything to do with you or your break-in. This was an isolated incident." He pulled on her hand, encouraging her to take a seat beside him.

"Did they find her attacker?"

"No," he admitted.

"Then it could have been the same person."

"There is the possibility, of course," he conceded. "But the MOs were different. From the looks of it, someone targeted Dawn Dyson specifically. They didn't take or disturb a thing. They broke in, beat her beyond recognition, and left without a trace. A client happened to stop by her house and found her."

"That's horrible. And—And I was so rude to her!" Laurel whispered.

"Hey, none of that." He hauled her into his arms and gave her a comforting squeeze. "You don't make a habit of being rude to people. I'm sure she did something to deserve it. Want to tell me about it?"

"Not really." She allowed herself to relax into his arms. "The last few days have been so crazy. . ."

"And I wasn't here for you." His voice was quiet with regret and self-derogation.

"You were working. And I had the Curly Girls and Boomer."

She felt him stiffen, regretting her words when he pulled away from her.

"Yeah. About this Boomer guy."

"Wh—What about him?"

"Who is he?"

"Just a guy from work."

"A guy who was there for you when I wasn't." He turned to her with a sulk. "A guy named *Boomer*? Seriously?"

Laurel chuckled at the expression on his face. "You saw him. It's not that he's fat. He's just... boom! Like six feet, fifteen, and at least three hundred pounds of solid muscle."

"He's not *that* tall," Cade contradicted. A smile played around the edges of his mouth as he playfully bumped his shoulder against hers. "And I could definitely take him, if it came down to that."

"It won't. Honestly. He's just a guy from work." With a truthful sigh, she picked up her wine glass and admitted, "A nice guy, but the one who required you to imitate my mom."

He stopped her with a knowing nod. "Yeah, I have one of those at my work, too. Only my guy is a girl."

A flash of jealousy stabbed through her, and she stiffened. "Oh, you do, do you?"

"Yeah, I do. And she can't seem to take the hint that I'm not interested."

"The thing is, I like Boomer. Over the course of the last few days, he's been a good friend to me, and he deserves more than just a 'thanks for all the help, now have a good life.' I feel like I owe him more than that."

Cade tensed. "How about a nice home-cooked dinner? Let me know when," he said dryly, "and I'll bring Amber along."

"Amber? Seriously? Her name is *Amber*?"

"Yeah," he said skeptically. "What's wrong with that?"

"They're always named Amber. Or Ashli, with an 'i.' Sometimes, they're a Felicia."

"Felicia?"

"Sometimes. Not always."

"Sometimes they're a Laurel," he added.

"No. Never a Laurel. Laurels aren't flashy enough."

"Flashy is overrated."

"Agreed. But they're never a Laurel."

"I'm lost. Who are 'they?'"

"The women who won't take no for an answer. The women who wear a man down, until finally it's easier to just go along with them than it is to resist their charms. They're the women who always get the guy."

"Not this guy. I honestly have never dated a woman by one of those names."

"So let me guess. Amber is tall and blonde, with killer legs up to here." She made an imaginary mark somewhere above her head.

"Close. Tall and sort of a strawberry-blonde, I'd say. And one of her legs is prosthetic."

"Oh. Oh, I—I wasn't expecting that."

"Hey, don't feel sorry for her. She's one of the most capable women I know and one heck of an officer. She despises pity, and frankly, she doesn't deserve it. She's sort of a badass if you want the truth. And totally cool. Easy on the eyes, too."

"So, why don't you want to date her?"

"Because I'm already in a relationship."

"You—You are?"

Cade took her wine glass from her and placed it on the table beside his own. "Let me rephrase that. I'd *like* to be in a relationship." His smile was soft, matching the look in his deliciously brown eyes. "With that Laurel chick I mentioned earlier."

She managed a light, if not somewhat breathless, reply. "Like you, I passed up the chick phase eight or ten years ago."

"Believe me," Cade said, his voice whiskey smooth, "I am well aware of the fact that you are a woman." He placed his hand on her knee again.

His eyes were too bright, and too deep, to stare into for long periods of time. If she did, Laurel knew she would become hopelessly lost. Now was the time to make her stand.

"What are we talking about here, Cade? What would a relationship between us even look like? Because, frankly, what we've been doing the past few months just isn't working for me."

"It isn't working for me, either," he admitted.

"Then why have we been doing this? Random dates here and there. Phone calls. A few kisses. Our new friends in The Sisters want the six of us to go out to eat again, but I can't speak for you. It's impossible to make future plans, because I don't know if we have a future."

He caught her hands in his, the hands she used in wild, exasperated gestures. "I know," Cade said. "And I'm sorry. In my own defense, I've been a fool."

She eyed him cautiously. "Your words, not mine."

"Look, we both know the score. We each have highly stressful, volatile careers. We're both dedicated to our careers. Careers that don't have a very good track record when it comes to long and lasting relationships." He looked down at their intertwined hands. "I guess... I guess I felt the odds were stacked against us. I felt defeated, before we even got started."

His admission surprised her. "I figured you for the kind of guy who welcomed a challenge."

He looked up with a rueful smile on his handsome face. "You sound like my mom. She reminded me of that very thing."

"So, what are you saying?"

"I'm saying I think it's worth the risk. *We're* worth the risk. No one is ever promised the future. Maybe the whole point is to grab what happiness you can when you can." He lifted one hand to her face, brushing the curve of her cheek with his finger. "I want to grab that happiness with you,

Laurel. Not with an Amber or an Ashli or a Felicia. With you."

"I—I think we could do that."

His eyes moved to the nervous smile working its way across her face. His gaze concentrated on her lips. "Yeah?" he whispered.

"Yeah."

He leaned in to kiss her, and Laurel felt happiness already blossoming inside. He pushed her gently back against the cushions, kissing her senseless.

He pulled away before the kiss became too heated. "Just to recap," he said, and she was pleased to hear the catch of breathlessness in his own husky voice, "you can now tell Boomer that you're definitely seeing someone. No more running bath water for you. If we can figure it out between our schedules—which is no small feat, as you well know—you can plan something with Genny and Cutter, and Madison and Brash. You'll take me to meet your parents, and you'll come with me to my party. Just know that if my little nieces and nephews tease me and ask if you're my 'girlfriend'," his voice held the same teasing inflection as kids on the playground used, "I plan to say yes." His dark eyes glittered.

"I like the sound of that," Laurel admitted, initiating the next kiss. Smiling against his lips, she asked, "So I guess that makes you my 'boyfriend,' huh?" She used the same inflection.

"I think that's the way this usually works."

Laurel pretended to think over his recap of their relationship rules. She tossed her dark curls to one side and determined, "I can work within those parameters."

The sassy little move left the side of her neck exposed. Cade nuzzled his face against it, kissing his way back to her eager lips. Their kisses were heating up when her phone buzzed on the coffee table.

They ignored the first few rings but knew it was only a delay tactic. In their careers, telephones needed answering.

"It's the hospital," she breathed, sparing it a glance. "I need to get this."

Cade sat up with a nod. At least it gave them a chance to catch their breaths and regain their bearings. The last few kisses had been intense.

Laurel answered her phone as she left the room, straightening her rumpled linen blouse as she went. Her cheeks were flushed a rosy red, and her lips were slightly swollen from his kisses. Cade's smile was shaky. He was certain he had never seen a more gorgeous woman in his life.

His smile faded as his own phone rang, flashing Chief Moore's personal number.

CHAPTER THIRTEEN

When Laurel returned to the living room a good ten minutes later, her cheeks were no longer rosy. In truth, they were downright ashen. Her legs wobbled a little as she walked, and it had nothing to do with the wine. The weakness in her knees wasn't even related to the scene she walked into, as endearing as it was; the handsome, rugged cowboy was cleaning up the remnants of their abandoned dinner.

Cade took one look at her and was instantly concerned. "Laurel?" he asked. "What is it?"

"That—That was my boss."

"Is something wrong? Do you have to go in to the hospital tonight?" Cade asked, bagging the last of the trash.

She shook her head, still in somewhat of a daze. "Quite the contrary," she said. She dropped onto the couch with a thud.

"What do you mean?"

"I... She said... That is, the directors feel..." Laurel stopped and started several times, unable to push the terrible words from her mouth.

Concerned, Cade stopped what he was doing and crouched in front of her. "Laurel? What is it, Lovely Laurel? You're as white as a ghost." He pushed a dark tendril away from her face, waiting for her to talk when she was ready.

"I—I've been suspended, pending the full investigation into Ylenia Tonchev's death!" The words burst from her, followed by a sob.

"Ah, darlin', I'm so sorry." He steadied himself on his bent toes as she leaned forward and rested her head on his shoulder. He wrapped his arms around her and let her cry.

"Eight years as a nurse and not a single blemish on my record! And now this!" she wailed.

"It's just a formality, darlin'. Hospital policy, I'm sure."

"They may just as well accuse me of killing that poor woman! I did nothing wrong, and yet they're punishing me."

"They're covering all their bases, Laurel. You know how these things go."

"Yes, I do!" When she jerked away, he took the opportunity to move, so that the circulation could return to his toes. He pivoted around and transferred to the couch beside her, while she threw her hands up in despair and went on a rant.

"Now the media will get wind of the suspension, and I'll be tried in the court of public opinion. My reputation will be in shreds. I'll be lucky to get a job in some hole-in-the-wall doctor's office. This is terrible. Terrible!"

"Come on, Laurel, it's not that bad." He tried pulling her back into his arms, but she resisted.

"Really? Have you ever been suspended?" she shot back.

"Actually, I have—officer-involved shooting. Twice. And I was absolved twice, just as you'll be." This time when he tugged, she came into his arms. "You've done nothing wrong, Laurel. It's just politics and posturing. The hospital has to appear impartial. They'll do their investigation, prove to the public that you're a devoted and honorable nurse, and that will be that."

"But what if it's not?"

"It will be."

After a long moment, Laurel sniffed and sat up. "I'm sorry. You don't know me very well, but I'm usually not like this. I don't normally cry so easily. But this... this is so personal, you know? It's an attack on my character. On my entire professional career and the very things I stand for. I've vowed to *save* lives, not take them!"

"You're right. I don't know you all that well— *yet*—" he was quick to point out, "but I did already know that about you. I also know you're a woman of impeccable character, and you have an amazing inner strength that will get you through this."

Laurel wiped the tears from her cheek. "You can change your mind, you know."

He cocked his blond head. "My mind?"

"About us being involved. I wouldn't blame you. Who wants their name linked to a possible murderer?"

He looked angered by the suggestion. "You really think I would dump you at a time like this?"

"Not dump me, exactly. Just decide it's too much, too soon. I mean, what? We've been in a relationship all of an hour, and already my name is about to be dragged through the mud. You're a police officer. You don't need the aggravation. I wouldn't blame you if you decided to put things on hold for a while."

"First of all, whether we admitted it or not, we've been caught in a relationship since our first run-in at the hospital." One corner of his mouth ticked up with a grudging half smile. "From the first time you stared me down with your flashing hazel eyes and gave me the what-for, I haven't been able to get you out of my head." He tilted her chin up so that she met his eyes and saw the words with her heart, not just heard them with her ears.

Laurel bit back a smile. She had mentally nicknamed him the Testosterone Man, comparing him to the old children's nursery rhyme. *Run, run, fast as you can. Gotta outrun the Testosterone Man.* Even from that very first day, she had been unable to resist the handsome but stubborn detective.

"Second of all, I don't scare so easily," he further informed her. "If *you've* changed *your* mind, that's one thing, but I've got sisters. I've seen girls cry before. A few tears and a little display of crazy won't chase me away."

Laurel sniffed again. "Good. Because talk like that may make me cry again."

"But there is something I have to tell you." The expression on his face told her it was serious.

Before he could say anything further, her doorbell rang. Almost simultaneously, her phone jingled. "This is Danni," she said, glancing at the screen. "She must already know. And my guess is that's Cami at the door."

"Should I get it?" he offered.

"Would you mind?"

"Not at all." He dropped a kiss onto the top of her head as he stood and as she answered the phone.

Like the cautious law officer he was, he checked the peephole before opening the door. Sure enough, a perky little blonde with ringlets stood on the other side. Her eyes widened when he swung the door open and invited her inside.

"Oh. I didn't realize Laurel had company. Should I come back?"

"Stay. She's expecting you."

"How? I hadn't planned to come over."

"Maybe it's that women's intuition thing you ladies have going on," he suggested. "That and just as the doorbell rang, Danni called. She figures word is out on the street already."

"I literally just heard. I hopped in the car and came right over." She closed the door behind her, asking, "So it's true?"

"The suspension? Yes. The guilt? No, of course not."

"I know that!" Cami said, propping her hands on her hips. Her eyes narrowed in suspicion. "Are you here to arrest her?"

"Of course not. We're having dinner."

"Oh." Her face brightened. "Like a date?"

"I guess you could call it that." Bracing himself for the playground jokes, he amended his answer. "Yes. Exactly like a date."

Cami grinned in approval and pranced into the living room. As Laurel ended her call, Cami engulfed her friend in a deep embrace. "It's going to be okay," she promised. "It will blow over soon."

"So do hurricanes," Laurel grumbled. "But they leave a path of destruction in their wake."

"Is Danni on the way over?"

"Yes. I told her it wasn't necessary, but she insisted."

"Of course she did. Hey, are those Layne's chicken fingers?"

"Yes. Help yourself," she said, even though Cami had done just that. "I've suddenly lost my appetite."

Cami swallowed, a guilty look on her face. "Should I put this back?"

"Of course not. Have all you want."

Cami looked to Cade for approval. "You done, too?"

"Yeah. Knock yourself out." He ran a hand through his short, blond hair. "Let me get you a glass for the wine."

"While you're in there, you may want to grab another bottle," Laurel advised. "In fact, bring two."

Under her breath, she added, "After all, I don't have to go to work tomorrow."

With Cade out of the room, Cami turned to her with a wide grin. "You two look cozy."

"It's been the one good thing to come of the day. Which reminds me, I need to call my parents."

"Being with Cade reminds you of your parents?" Cami looked a bit mortified. "Please, no details."

Laurel almost laughed, but her mother's phone was already ringing on the other end, and her news was anything but funny.

By the time Cade returned with wine glasses for the Curly Girls, two more bottles of wine, and a box of party crackers he had found, Laurel was done filling in her parents.

"Good news," she said with a false smile. "You're going to meet the family sooner than expected. They've been at a reunion but are leaving first thing in the morning. They should be here around noon."

Cade took a seat beside her and pulled her under his arm. "From the frying pan into the fire, huh?"

"Not the way I would have planned it, but it is what it is," she murmured.

When the doorbell rang, Cami motioned for them to stay seated. "Don't part on my account," she teased. "I'm sure it's Danni."

Laurel turned her face up to Cade's. "You've certainly made her night."

"Hmm. I'm more concerned about making your night, than hers."

"You've made mine, too. Thank you for being here," she said with sincerity. "Thank you for insisting on sticking it out, even if—"

"Quit while you're ahead, Lovely Laurel," he advised. "And if seeing me put my arm around you makes her happy, imagine how thrilled we'll all be when I do this." He touched her face with gentle fingers and lowered his head for a slow and thorough kiss.

A loud stage whisper interrupted them. "I think they've forgotten we're here," Cami said in amusement.

"Shall we wait in the kitchen?" Danni whisper-shouted back.

To their delight, Laurel raised a finger to indicate she needed one more minute. Drawing the kiss to a reluctant end, she met Cade's amused eyes, gave him one more quick peck, and motioned her friends forward.

"I rushed over thinking I would find you in tears and instead, I find you in the arms of a hot guy!" Danni chided playfully.

"The day didn't turn out all bad," Laurel agreed. "But there have been tears."

"We decided to go for the shock treatment," Cade joked. "The good, the bad, and the ugly, all at once."

"You're calling our friend ugly?" Cami demanded.

"Never. I'm calling the situation ugly. Here, ladies, have some wine."

"I like him already." Danni smirked, accepting the proffered glass.

After their initial laughter, they settled in for a serious conversation. They rehashed events and scenarios, catching Cade up to speed on hospital gossip and observations they had made.

"I can't help but feel Trevor set me up," Laurel said.

"Why do you say that?" Cami asked.

"He graced me with his presence today while I was on my lunch break. He accused me of selling him out to the police. He ranted first about me, then about Dr. Ainsley. He said he had a meeting with Director Gaines this afternoon. I have no doubt he fed them plenty of accusations about me and made me look as guilty as possible."

"What's this about Dr. Ainsley? I know the two of them don't seem to get along very well, but what was he ranting about?" Danni wanted to know.

"According to him, she had more reason to kill the professor than anyone. Some crazy theory about her wanting to buy the professor's house. He overheard the doctor telling her agent she would do *anything* to get her hands on it."

Cade frowned. "That's a big leap. 'Anything' doesn't usually include murder."

"What I said. But this is Trevor we're talking about. I seriously think the man is unhinged." She relayed the incident at the grocery store and the man's transformation from rage to casual conversation.

"And he seriously didn't remember the chainsaw patient?"

"Not at all."

"You're certain he was the attending nurse?"

Laurel closed her eyes, thinking back to that night. "Yes. He took the ambulance, I took the professor's call. I even saw him returning to the room, just before I delivered the blanket to the professor."

"Wait. This Winslow guy was in the hall?" Cade asked.

"Yes. There was a lot going on at the moment. Boomer came around the corner with a crash cart, Trevor brushed past me with something in his hand, and there was general chaos at the end of the hall."

"So, Winslow *could* have gone into the professor's room, and no one would have seen him."

"It's definitely possible," Laurel agreed.

"He was in 10 at least part of the time," Danni countered. "It was all hands on deck, so I was there helping. I saw Nurse Winslow in there."

"But he stepped out at some point. I saw him."

Cade looked thoughtful. "Tell me more about Dr. Ainsley."

"She's a senior physician at the hospital. She'd had a long and impressive career here in the twin cities. Her husband is a professor at the university."

"Therefore, it stands to reason she could have known Professor Tonchev through her husband and had been to her home before."

Laurel looked at her newly minted boyfriend with obvious doubt. "What? You think she became obsessed with the house?"

Cade shrugged. "If Winslow's account of the facts is to be believed, it sounds entirely possible."

"That's a big if," Cami reminded him.

"Does the doctor have a temper?"

"Ainsley? She's as docile as a lamb," Danni claimed.

"That's… not entirely so," Laurel corrected her friend.

"Come on. You can't base a thing on Trevor's rantings!"

"I witnessed it myself. In all the hubbub yesterday, I didn't tell y'all everything. Dawn's visit put me in such a bad mood, I just didn't want to talk about it."

"You mean after your thirty-minute rant," Danni said with a cheeky grin.

"Right. After that. But Monica Ainsley showed up here shortly after we hung up, apparently under the impression that my house was for sale. She was terribly embarrassed when she found out her error and, judging from the call I overheard on her way out the door, more than a little irate at Dawn for deceiving her."

"In case you haven't already heard," Cade said, addressing Laurel's two friends, "now may be a good time to mention that Dawn Dyson was found beaten in her home during the overnight hours. She's in serious condition at *Methodist*."

Both women were shocked. "What! The news mentioned something about a home invasion and assault, but they didn't name names."

"Are you saying Dr. *Ainsley* could have done this?" Cami asked incredulously.

Cade remained unbiased. "I'm just stating facts." He shot Laurel a glance, hesitated, and made an obvious decision to continue. "There's something else, Laurel. I didn't get a chance to tell you earlier."

"That's right," she remembered with a nod. "We were interrupted by the doorbell."

"Chief Moore wouldn't tell me much, but he made a personal effort to give me a head's up on what was happening." He took her hand in his and looked her in the eye, giving it to her straight. "He told me you've been named the top suspect in the murder of Professor Tonchev."

Laurel was too stunned to reply, but her friends had plenty of objections on her behalf. She gripped Cade's hand and stared at a spot on the hardwood floor, her vision blurring with unshed tears.

When she finally spoke, she asked in a quiet voice, "Did he say why?"

"He did. This goes no further than this room. Swear to me." He pinned each woman with his sharp gaze, waiting for their solemn vows before continuing. "Apparently, an anonymous source turned in a key piece of evidence earlier today. Your fingerprints were on it."

"But what was it?" Danni asked. "The professor was strangled. I saw the bruising on her neck myself."

"Again, this goes no further than this room."

Again, a round of murmured agreements.

"Upon further examination, the coroner was able to identify another impression, other than that of the killer's fingers. Apparently, the professor was wearing—"

He didn't need to finish. Laurel knew what he was about to say.

"A necklace," she whispered.

"I'm afraid so," he confirmed, again squeezing her hand.

"It makes sense now. That's what the break-ins were about! Somehow, the killer knew I had the necklace. He or she must have slipped it into my pocket and then broke into my house, hoping to steal it back."

"What necklace?" Cami asked, totally lost.

"There was another break in?" Danni asked.

Laurel gave her friends a quick rundown of the events surrounding finding, forgetting, and hiding the necklace, only to have it stolen.

"Of course it had my fingerprints on it," Laurel said. "I handled it several times. And I would have handled it again today when I turned it into lost and found, but it was already gone."

Trying to get it straight in her mind, Danni clarified, "So the killer broke back into your house on Sunday night and stole it from your secret hiding spot?"

"It was hardly a secret," she scoffed. "They sell jewelry boxes like mine every day, and I'm sure they all have the 'hidden' drawer. But yes, it looks that way."

"Trevor!" Danni said. "He probably took the necklace to the police!"

Cade twisted his mouth in thought. "Not necessarily," he said.

"Huh? What do you mean?"

"Didn't you say Dr. Ainsley treated herself to a self-guided tour of your house yesterday?"

"Yes, but—" She stopped mid-sentence, remembering how the doctor had been gone from the room longer than expected. She clamped her mouth shut, amending her answer to a simple, "Yes."

"You need to call the police and file another breaking and entering complaint. You need to tell them that this time, something was taken. A necklace."

"But—"

"No buts. You need to go on record as reporting the necklace stolen before they use it against you as evidence."

"But Chief Moore—"

"Doesn't know I was here," he finished for her. "And you won't mention that fact to the police when they arrive. I'll be long gone by then, but your friends will be here to back you up. Do you understand what I'm telling you?"

"To lie?"

"No. Whatever you do, don't lie to the police. But in this case, and just this once, you don't have to volunteer unnecessary details."

Dazed, Laurel stared at him in utter shock. "Where is Detective Cade Resnick and what have you done to him?"

Cupping her face with his large hand, his lopsided smile was bittersweet. "Tonight, I'm not a detective. I'm just a man trying to protect his girlfriend, the only way he knows how."

CHAPTER FOURTEEN

Just before leaving that evening, Cade stole a moment alone with Laurel.

"There's one other thing, Lovely Laurel, and this may be the hardest of all."

"Harder than telling me I'm the lead suspect in a murder investigation?" She snorted. "I somehow doubt it."

"It's harder for me, at any rate. I want you to know this isn't my idea, and not one I like. But as much as it pains me to say it, I do agree it's the best way."

"Stop stalling," she said irritably, "and just say it!"

"Captain Moore strongly suggested I keep my distance from you during the investigation. And by *strongly suggest*, he basically meant it as a command."

Laurel looked stricken. "But—"

"I know," he told her solemnly, gathering her into his arms. "I told you I would be here for you, and now I'm being forced to abandon you. But the chief is right, you know. The media would have a field day exploiting our relationship and the department's bias toward you."

"I—I understand," she claimed. Intellectually, she knew he had a point. But her heart had trouble following along.

"This isn't something I want, Lovely Laurel. I want to be here for you. I want to prove I meant it earlier when I said I wouldn't tuck tail and run. Please. You have to know this isn't by choice."

One look into his brown eyes, and she knew he spoke from the heart.

"It's not something either of us chooses, nor likes," she agreed, touching her hand to his chest. "But the captain is right. This could not only reflect poorly on the department—"

He broke in with an adamant, "I'm not concerned about the department's reputation! I'm worried about yours!"

"I know. And I truly appreciate that. But the two go hand in hand. If people think I'm getting special treatment from the police, they'll be more apt to believe I'm guilty. And the DA's office could feel pressured into proving a point." It hurt to say the words, but Laurel nodded her dark curls and whispered, "The captain's right. You have to keep your distance."

Cade closed his eyes, resigning himself to the inevitable. "The captain likes you, Laurel. He likes *us*. He has too much integrity to give you special treatment, but he has more than enough to make sure this investigation is handled in a fair and comprehensive manner. He won't allow Castilleja or anyone else to jump to conclusions or make an early arrest. He'll make sure you're proved innocent."

"Thank you. I'll keep that in mind."

"Keep this is mind, too." He pulled her close and lowered his head for a long, thorough kiss. It held more promise than it did heat.

"I should go," he said at last.

"I know."

They lingered for one more kiss, then another. Laurel was the first to break contact and step out of his arms.

It broke her heart, watching her boyfriend transform back into the detective.

"You need to call the department and make a report, as soon as I walk out the door. Tell them you debated on whether or not to call, searching every place you thought it could be, before realizing someone had taken it."

"I will."

"I'm not sure how much we'll be able to talk. Between closing in on an arrest for this other case, and the potential for someone peeking into our phone records. . ."

"I hadn't thought of that," she murmured, paling. *Now she couldn't even* talk *to him?* This night just kept getting worse!

"We'll figure out a way, Lovely Laurel," he assured her. "We'll get through this."

She offered a shaky smile. "Together, even if they keep us apart?"

His warm gaze was determined. "Together," he insisted.

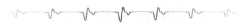

Cami and Danni were by her side when the police arrived. To Laurel's immense relief, even after thirty minutes of intense grilling, there was no need to lie; Cade's name was never mentioned.

"You'll come home with me tonight," Danni informed her.

At best, Laurel's protest was half-hearted. "It's not necessary."

"I say it is."

Her friend didn't say it in so many words, but Laurel knew the reason. Cami was working tomorrow, while Danni— and now herself— were off. This was the best solution for everyone and didn't leave time for Laurel to wallow in self-pity.

Despite it being a short night, Laurel barely slept. She tossed and turned until the sun came up just a few hours later. A shower and hot coffee did little to revive her. Both her mind and her heart were heavy. Low spirits rounded out the depressing trio.

With nothing better to do, Laurel went home and decided to pursue her own theories of who might have killed the professor. With no information on patients and guests in the ER at the time of the crime, she concentrated on hospital personnel.

While any one of them had the opportunity to strangle the victim, only two had possible

motive. It seemed unlikely that Doctor Ainsley
would have killed her for an off-chance opportunity
to buy her house, but she couldn't let her bias
toward Trevor color her judgment. Even though he
had opportunity (she had seen him in the hallway
immediately before discovering the professor) and
motive (he had an overall disdain for women in
authority, plus a previous connection through his
ex-wife) she couldn't definitively place him at her
house. The only possibility was that he had broken
in, which she couldn't prove.

Laurel took notes in a spiral notebook,
making charts of possible timelines and
opportunities. The exercise made good use of her
afternoon and offered a distraction for her troubled
mind, but in the end, it did little to prove her
suspicions.

Her parents arrived back in town around
noon. Having their unerring support helped bolster
her spirits, but too many hugs and such close
attention became stifling. It was a dirty trick on her
part, but Laurel requested some of her mother's
special pot roast, knowing she would go home and
cook for the rest of the day.

To please her parents, Laurel agreed to
dinner at their house, followed by a pajama party.
As she packed yet another overnight bag, she
fought off a sense of battle fatigue. The worst part
was knowing that, if no other suspects came to
light, the nightmare could just be beginning.

Laurel locked the door behind her and threw
her bag into the car. She inadvertently knocked

over a half-filled cup in her cupholder, the remnants of her last visit to a drive-through restaurant. The sticky soft drink spilled into her floorboard and brought a disgruntled moan from her lips.

"Great. Just great!" she muttered.

She returned to the house for paper towels and a soapy rag to tackle the worst of it.

Still at the sink as she wet the cloth, Laurel froze when she heard a familiar voice behind her.

"Knock, knock."

She turned around with a startled expression.

"Tr—Trevor. What—What are you doing here?"

"The door was opened. I let myself in."

Stupid, Laurel! She chided herself. Stupid, stupid, stupid.

"You weren't at work today," Trevor went on needlessly, "even though you were on the schedule."

"There was a last-minute change," she answered, her tone evasive.

"I thought you should know," the man informed her. "The hospital grapevine says you've been arrested for the death of Professor Tonchev."

Laurel sucked in a sharp breath. "As usual," she said as nonchalantly as possible, "the grapevine is wrong. I haven't been arrested."

Yet. She added the small but significant clarification to herself.

She watched nervously as he continued to approach the bar. The bar where her notebook rested. The notebook that clearly had his name in it, circled in red. He was her most likely candidate as a murderer.

She needed to get him away from the bar and out of her house, as soon as possible.

"I appreciate you stopping by to check on me," she went on, trying to sound light and airy. "But as you can see, it wasn't necessary. The rumors are false."

Laurel did her best to keep her eyes off the incriminating notebook. The last thing she wanted to do was to make the man angry. Even if he wasn't a murderer, he was unstable. He had a legendary temper and was known for throwing quite the tantrum when incensed.

Trevor didn't take the hint and offer to leave. Laurel was torn, deciding which was better: to stay in place and use the bar as some small means of safety and separation, or to come around the counter and block his view of her handwritten notes.

She must have inadvertently glanced at the notebook. The breath stilled in her lungs when she saw his eyes follow.

"Why is my name written on that paper?" he asked in suspicion.

"Just—Just making sure we were adequately staffed before I called in sick," she lied, making a grab for the book.

She wasn't quick enough. Trevor snagged the spiral notebook and looked at it, his eyes widening when he saw her notes and his own name circled in red.

"You think *I* killed the professor?" His voice was incredulous.

That massive ego of his! It was all Laurel could do not to roll her eyes. I'm sure it never occurred to him that someone might question the almighty Trevor Winslow for something as undignified as murder.

"No." Even in her own ears, the denial sounded weak.

"You do!" he cried. "You think I did this!"

Laurel expected to see rage in his eyes. Instead, she saw nothing but confusion.

"Why would I want to kill the professor?" he asked, clearly perplexed.

"I have no idea," she lied again.

He glanced down at the notes. "Because of Marissa? That doesn't even make sense!"

"You—You never mentioned you already knew the professor. That she and your ex-wife were good friends."

"How would that give me motive to do something as despicable as kill someone?"

His befuddled look caused her to tip her hand. She hadn't meant to confess all, but he looked so confused, she felt the need to explain. "You may have blamed her for splitting up your marriage. She may have encouraged Marissa to leave you."

"*I* left Marissa," he told her haughtily. "I will not tolerate a liar and a cheat."

"She cheated on you?" That would explain some of the bitterness.

"Of course not!" Again, that ego. With an insulted sniff, he informed her, "I discovered she was accepting bribes to give students a passing grade. Marissa has a weakness for shopping, and I had cut off her allowance."

"Her *allowance*?" Laurel cried in shock. Leave it to Trevor to be so chauvinistic as to give his wife an 'allowance' as if she were a child, and not his partner in life.

"That's right, her allowance. And what of it?" he asked nastily.

Careful not to anger him, Laurel stammered, "I—I was just surprised."

"She was terrible at managing money. An allowance was the only way to keep her spending in line."

Laurel flashed the palms of her hands. "Hey. I'm not judging you."

Not entirely true, but far be it from her to say so. The man was unstable.

"You still haven't explained what my motive for murder could possibly be. The professor and I were working together to get Marissa help with her shopping addiction and to keep the sordid details of the grading scandal from coming out."

"Oh." Laurel was too stunned to think of a better reply.

"But I do think you're on the right track," he said. He dropped the notebook to the counter and tapped on the other name she had written. "I think Dr. Ainsley could have done it."

"It doesn't make sense. . ."

"But I did? You thought I was capable of murder, but not the good doctor?" he challenged.

"I've already told you. She coveted the professor's house. She said she would do anything to get it."

From the adjoining dining room, another voice spoke. "I know that's right."

"Boomer?" Laurel asked, jerking her gaze up to the blond giant. Even though Trevor had done nothing to threaten her, she felt a huge sense of relief at having an ally show up at this critical moment.

"Sorry. The door was open, and I heard voices. Are we having a work party, and someone forget to invite me?"

"Hardly a party," Trevor said dryly. "Your girlfriend here is accusing me of murder."

Ever the one to lighten a mood, Boomer asked in a nonchalant manner, "Who'd you kill?"

"No one! But Nurse Benson is trying to pin the professor's murder on me, simply because my ex-wife was her TA."

"Huh. Small world, ain't it?" He didn't seem the least bit concerned about the first part of the other man's comment.

"Jest all you like. I refuse to stand here and be insulted like this! I'm leaving."

"Close the door on your way out, will you, buddy?" Boomer asked, not bothering to look over his shoulder at the nurse's retreating back.

When Trevor was gone, Laurel sagged against the counter in relief. "I am so glad to see you!" she declared, putting a hand over her pumping heart. "I didn't know how he would react."

"To what?"

"I—I had a theory. A weak one, granted, but a theory he inadvertently discovered. I entertained the notion that Trevor may have killed the professor."

Boomer laughed at the thought. "That wimp? It takes real strength to strangle a person. He couldn't even hold a pillow over someone's face, much less get a good enough grip to strangle them by the throat." He put his hand on his own throat to demonstrate.

Three long, slender scrapes drew Laurel's attention. They looked like those left by a cat's claws but wider. *More like a woman's nails,* Laurel thought, wondering idly if Boomer had a new girlfriend.

From the looks of it, she amended with an amused smile, *I'd guess he doesn't anymore. Those look more like defensive wounds from a fight. And they look fresh.*

She couldn't say why, but the thought was instantly sobering.

Not because she was interested in Boomer for herself.

Not even because she considered him a friend and didn't want to see him hurt in a relationship.

Laurel couldn't quite put a finger on her unease, however. Something nagged at the back of her mind, but it remained just beyond her grasp.

Changing the subject, she asked, "What brings you by today, Boomer?"

"Is it true?" he asked, the expression in his eyes dark. "Did the hospital suspend you?"

"Is—Is that what they said?" she countered.

"Not officially. Officially, you called in sick. But everyone is saying they put you on administrative leave, pending an arrest in the prof's murder."

"I wish I could say it's just rumor. . ." She dropped her gaze, too ashamed to look her friend in the eye.

"You're freaking kidding me, right? They're honestly punishing you for an ongoing police investigation?" He sounded angrier than she had ever heard him. Apparently, even the easygoing tech had a temper when riled.

"It would seem so," she murmured.

"This isn't right! They can't do that to you!"

"Thanks for sticking up in my defense, but obviously they can." Her smile was wan. "I know I can't take it personally. They're simply doing their job. This will all blow over soon. The police will arrest someone else for murder, and I'll be back on the job in no time."

"Do they have a suspect?"

"I have no idea."

"Your cowboy doesn't have an inside track on the investigation?"

"Even if he did, it's hardly something he would discuss with me."

"He didn't stay long the other night." Boomer smirked. "Trouble in paradise?"

Laurel cocked her head in confusion. "How would you know how long he did or didn't stay? I heard you roar off."

He looked sheepish. "I admit to circling the block, making certain he didn't cause a scene."

If she needed to create the illusion that she and Cade were no longer involved, she may as well start here. "He didn't. We, uh, decided to cool things for a while. He decided being associated with me was bad for his image." She studied her fingernails, so the lie was more believable.

"You're kidding, right?"

"I'm afraid not. You can take that back to the gossip mill with you," Laurel volunteered. "My life is officially in the gutter. Shunned by the hospital *and* the detective."

"Hey, I can rough 'em up for you, if you want me to," Boomer offered in jest. "I know for a fact you're innocent. The hospital has no right judging you like that, and neither does the detective!" He grew more indignant as he spoke. "That goes to show how much the stupid police knows. And they call him their top detective?"

Laurel felt the need to defend Cade to the suddenly scornful man. "He's not assigned to this case."

"Good, because he can't see what's right in front of his face."

It could have been a compliment.

He could have referred to Cade dumping her, unable to see the wonderful woman that was right in front of him.

But Laurel didn't think so.

Something else niggled her mind, accompanying her unease upon seeing the fresh claw marks. Upon seeing this angry, vindictive side of her friend. He pretended to joke about getting even and roughing up anyone who doubted her, but something about his words—about his tone, and that dark look in his eyes— told her it wasn't all in jest.

Laurel didn't like this newly exposed Boomer. She wasn't sure why, but she suddenly wasn't comfortable in his presence. She felt claustrophobic with the big man taking up so much space in her kitchen.

"Boomer, I hate to be rude, but my parents are expecting me for dinner."

His eyes narrowed in suspicion. "I thought your parents were out of town."

"They came in this morning. At my request, Mom's making pot roast." She flashed him a smile. "You should taste it. It's divine."

"Is that an invitation?"

A CASE OF STRANGULATION *by A Stranger*

"No!" She caught herself, realizing how horrified she must have sounded. "Uh, I mean, no. Not tonight. I'm really not up for company. I'm sure you understand."

"Not really. I thought we were friends."

"We are!" she assured him in haste. She didn't want to stir his ire again. She liked the jovial, easygoing Boomer much better than the quick-tempered one. "But it's been a rough week, and my parents are just getting back from a trip. None of us are going to be good company tonight. I plan to eat and hit the sack. In fact, my things are already in the car. Want to walk me out?"

"Why are you acting weird all of a sudden?"

She knew her movements were jerky. She knew her voice was stiff. She couldn't explain her unease, but it was there all the same. She clung to her mantra that only told half the story. "Like I told you, it's been a long week."

"I'd like to meet your parents."

Laurel nibbled at her lower lip in worry. Somehow, the words sounded like an order. A borderline threat of some kind.

She chided herself for overreacting. Don't be ridiculous! This is Boomer we're talking about. Good ole', easygoing Boomer. Your friend. Everyone's friend.

"Another time," she promised. She kept walking, leading the way to the door.

She had just opened it when he grabbed her arm roughly and said in a low voice, "Now."

CHAPTER FIFTEEN

Of all people to come to her rescue, Trevor Winslow was the least likely hero candidate of all. But she opened the door, and there he was again, his face contorted in an angry glare.

"Tr—Trevor!"

"What are you doing here, Winslow?" Boomer barked.

Ignoring the other man's snarl, Trevor addressed Laurel. "I was so angry at your outrageous and unfounded accusations, I almost forgot what I came for. Director Gaines asked that I collect your keys to anything hospital related. They've named me as acting head nurse in your absence." He gave her a superior sniff.

Laurel had a moment of doubt. Earlier, he had seemed so genuinely stupefied by her accusations that she had grudgingly believed him. But had this been some nefarious plot by him, after all? Perhaps not to get even with the professor as she first thought. Perhaps it was to get even with her and to take her place at *Texas General*. It sounded like something the man was capable of.

"They, uh, are in my purse," she said, her mind awhirl. *How was this happening?* Her mind screamed. *They're taking my keys. My reputation. My world as I know it.* Laurel cleared the emotions from her throat before continuing, "In the car. I'll go get them."

When she would have pulled out of his hold, Boomer threw his arm around her shoulders in an overly familiar gesture. The weight bore down on her petite shoulders. "We'll get them," he corrected. "We're headed out to her car right now."

This was her chance to put distance between herself and both men. At this point, Laurel wasn't comfortable around either one of them.

"You two stay here. I'll just be a minute."

Boomer persisted. "We're headed to your parents for dinner, remember? It's easiest if I just ride with you. Trevor, walk us out to the car, and you can get the keys there."

Laurel wasn't sure if this was some crazy macho thing Boomer had going on, or not. Maybe he was trying to assert his place in her life and make it appear they were more than just friends. Then again, maybe he was subtly forcing himself on her, insisting he be by her side whether she wanted him there or not.

She didn't. And it was high time to set him straight.

She intended to give his hand upon her shoulder a pointed look and then pierce him with her own laser-sharp eyes as she firmly asked him to remove his arm.

Instead, her eyes fell upon the scrape marks again, and realization rolled over her.

Unbidden, the scenes played out like movie snippets in her mind.

Boomer, passing her in the hallway just before she discovered the professor dead, a grim expression on his face. Coming from the direction of the professor's room.

Boomer, brushing against her at the professor's door, his hand within inches of her scrubs' pocket.

Boomer, showing up at her house uninvited, immediately before her house was broken into the first time.

Boomer, showing up afterwards, miraculously hearing about the incident even when few others had. So eager to help clean every room of her house. So eager to share his own secret hiding places, in hopes of learning hers.

Boomer, so insisted that she stay with Cami on Sunday night, the night the rug had been mysteriously straightened.

Boomer, surprised to hear about Dawn's after-hours visit to the late professor's house.

Dawn, attacked and beaten in her bed that very night.

Boomer, mentioning he dabbled in real estate. Advising her to speak with him when and if she ever listed her house.

Boomer, oddly offended when he made his statement about not pushing around hospital equipment for the rest of his life.

Dr. Ainsley, mentioning giving a new agent a chance at her business. A male agent.

Boomer, calling off work with car trouble yesterday, the day after Dawn's attack. And now something that looked suspiciously like defensive wounds upon his beefy hands, still fresh and raw.

Boomer.

Laurel swallowed hard and tried collecting her thoughts. Keeping her voice as steady as possible, she looked to the other nurse for help.

"Trevor, I'm actually glad you came back." She willed the tremble from her voice. "If you're taking over for me for a few days, there's a few things we need to go over. Maybe we should go inside and discuss this." She managed to free herself from Boomer, pushing dark curls from her face without quite meeting his eyes. "Boomer, this will probably just bore you. I appreciate you stopping by but like I said, it's been a long week. I know you understand." She offered a half smile, trying to sell the lie.

Laurel punched in her door code, careful to shield the keypad from prying eyes. She all but pulled Trevor inside and followed quickly behind, intending to close the door between them and the tech.

For a man his size, Boomer was quick. He pushed his way inside, causing the door to bang back against the wall.

Nearby, a framed print teetered and fell to the floor.

He barged in behind them, his voice a bellow. "Understand? *Understand?*" he demanded. "What's to understand? That you're both registered nurses, and I'm just a lowly patient tech? Is *that* what you're saying, Laurel?"

Before Laurel could find her voice and protest, Trevor did the unthinkable. He stood up for her.

"Now see here!" he said in a stern voice, bowing up to a man who was taller, bigger, and clearly stronger than he.

"That's enough out of you, *nursie!*" With no less effort than he would use to swat a fly, Boomer backhanded the other man, almost knocking him off his feet.

Laurel found her voice, along with her temper. ""Boomer! Stop this! What has gotten into you?"

He turned on her, his green eyes bleary with rage. "I thought you were different, Laurel," he spat in disappointment. "I thought you could see beyond the labels and the pay grade. But you're just like all the rest. You think you're better than the rest of us. The rest of us who aren't born with silver spoons in our mouths and didn't get some fancy medical degree at some fancy university. You think dating a patient tech is beneath you."

"That's not true, Boomer, and you know it."

"Then why wouldn't you go out with me?" he demanded, thrusting his face uncomfortably close to hers.

Now wasn't the time to split hairs, but Laurel found herself pointing out, "For one thing, you never actually asked."

He pulled back a margin, looking puzzled. "I asked if you wanted to catch a game."

She propped her hands upon her hips. "That's hardly the same as asking a girl out on a date."

"If I had, would you have said yes?" he challenged.

She couldn't lie about this. "Probably not."

"See?" His cry was triumphant and more than just a bit wild. He threw out his arms with an emphatic gesture. "That's why I did it! I was trying to better myself! I was trying to up my station in life, so you would give me a second look and agree to go out with me!"

He wasn't making sense. Laurel tried reasoning with him, even though the gleam in his eyes was becoming increasingly wild. "Boomer, it has nothing to do with your station in life. I wouldn't have gone out with you because I was already involved with someone else."

"Oh, yes," he sneered, "I know all about it. The cowboy detective. I'm sure he makes more money than a patient tech and a real estate agent, combined!"

Laurel frowned. "Real estate agent?" she asked.

Belatedly, she recalled the movie snippet about Dr. Ainsley giving a new agent a chance to earn her business.

All the images came back now, playing out at warp speed.

"Boomer," she said, her voice coming out shaky and breathless. "What—What have you done?" She stepped back, edging closer to Trevor. His face had gone pale.

"Do you have any idea how hard it is to get a leg up in this business?" Boomer ranted. "It's all about connections. You have to know somebody. I spent every waking hour, and every day off, studying until my eyes were crossed. It took me longer than most, but I finally earned my real estate license. And still, no one would hire me." Telling the story aloud made him even angrier. His face turned a mottled red. "I didn't have the right look. I didn't have the right friends. I needed experience. I needed a letter of recommendation. I needed something to prove I could be as good as anyone else in the business." He leaned in so close, Laurel could feel his hot breath on her skin. He stabbed a beefy finger into his chest, his face consorting with rage. "I. Wasn't. Good. Enough."

"I—I'm sure that's not so, Boomer," she mumbled.

"One agent finally promised to give me a chance. *IF.*"

"If?" Laurel wasn't certain she wanted to know the answer.

"If I could secure a client on my own, he would hire me."

Laurel had a terrible idea where his tale was heading. She shook her head to stop him.

"Look, Boomer. You don't have to tell us this. And my parents are waiting supper on me. . ."

"Is my work not as important as yours?" he snarled. "Not as interesting?"

Rousing up the courage to speak, Trevor cleared his throat and agreed with Laurel. "She— She's right. As interesting as it is, you don't have to tell us all this. It's hardly our field. And a very complex one, from what I understand." He flashed a cheesy smile. "Above my head, to be truthful."

Boomer's laugh was bitter. "Now I know you're lying. You're arrogant enough to believe *nothing* is above your head. You overplayed your hand, nursie."

From the side of her mouth, Laurel hissed, "He's right."

Another swing from Boomer's hand, and the male nurse landed on the floor. Trevor cowered there, making no attempt to get up.

This time, Boomer's laugh was real. Malicious, but real.

"Yeah, I thought so," he scoffed. "Nothing but a pansy. Too weak and sniveling to do something as strenuous as strangle someone." His face contorted with anger. "But you didn't have a problem with stealing, did you? You took the necklace!"

"N—Necklace?" Trevor rubbed his jaw.

"The necklace! The necklace you somehow took from my truck. Gold chain? Antique pendant? Does that ring a bell?"

Looking clueless, Trevor admitted, "I found one like that in the parking lot. It looked like the one the professor wore, so I turned it in the police."

"You *what?*" Boomer shrieked. "You stupid idiot!" He kicked at the man with his size-twelve shoe, but Trevor rolled just enough to avoid the blow.

Laurel stood back in horror as it all became clear to her. For whatever reason, Boomer had strangled the professor. When he realized his prints were on the chain she wore, he jerked it from her neck and hid the evidence at the first opportunity. Laurel's pocket had soon provided that opportunity. He then broke into her house—repeatedly, so it seemed—until he found it. Instead of stashing it in his favorite box of 'poison,' he kept it in his truck before dropping it in the hospital parking lot. It seemed Trevor had been the one to turn it in to the police, after all, but not for the reason she first believed.

"Why, Boomer?" The whispered question was pulled from Laurel. She didn't want to know the truth, but she *needed* to. She needed to understand how this man—*her friend*—could do something as heinous as murder someone. "What did the professor ever do to you?"

"This had nothing to do with the professor," he claimed. "She was a complete stranger to me. But I had heard Dr. Ainsley mention her name, and I knew how desperate she was to buy her house. I approached the professor with an offer. Above market price. It was a sweet deal, but she all but laughed in my face. Made some snide remark about coming to the hospital to be treated, not harassed."

Laurel stared at her former friend with horror. "So, you just strangled her?"

"Not at first. I tried reasoning with her. It was the perfect deal. She would make a nice profit, Doctor A would have the house she wanted, and I would have experience and my own deal to bring to the hiring table. But *noo*." Boomer drew the word out sarcastically. "She wouldn't hear of it. She threatened to turn me in to the hospital *and* to the real estate board! My whole future would be ruined. All my hard work. That just wouldn't do. That wouldn't do, at all." His face set into hard, bitter lines. "I did what I had to do to shut her up."

Behind him, another voice spoke. Cade stood in the open doorway, his service revolver drawn.

"That's all I needed to hear. George 'Boomer' Scott, you are under arrest for the murder of Ylenia Tonchev."

Boomer's eyes widened in surprise. "You set me up?" he cried, looking at Laurel in utter disbelief.

"No! I didn't even know he was there."

But thank God he was!

"It doesn't matter, Scott. I heard your confession." Cade produced a pair of handcuffs as behind him, sirens wailed, and two police cars careened to a stop in a kaleidoscope of red and blue strobe lights.

Trevor spoke from his place on the floor, flashing his phone. "And I have it on recording."

Boomer knew it was over. He gave Laurel another long, sorrowful look, before hanging his blond head in regret. "It could have been sweet. I was going to make something of myself."

Laurel made no reply. She watched in stunned silence as Cade snapped the handcuffs into place, the cold, hard steel biting into Boomer's wrists as the blond giant's arms were wrenched behind him. Uniformed police swarmed into her house. The sound of rushing feet, blaring radios, and barked orders resounded within the walls and echoed in her head. Boomer was hauled off to the squad car, and Trevor was hauled up off the floor.

Uncaring of who saw them, Cade engulfed Laurel into his arms. "It's over, Laurel," he said into her dark curls.

"B—B—But... How did you. . ." She couldn't form a coherent sentence as her face buried into his shoulder.

"I didn't," he said, sensing her question. "I didn't know."

"Then, why were you here?"

"I told you, Lovely Laurel. I'm always watching out for you." He stroked the back of her head, soothing her with the repetitive motion.

The waver in her voice exposed her broken heart. "He killed her, Cade. He strangled her so he could make a commission on her house! How— How horrible is that?"

"Shh, now," he urged in a soft voice. "It's over now."

She wormed her arms around his waist and tightened them in a squeeze. "I'm as hurt as I am mad," she confessed. "He was my friend, and he used me. Far worse than that, he killed an innocent woman and most likely attacked Dawn Dyson."

"The good news is that Dawn is expected to survive. She has a long road of recovery in front of her, but she should heal with time."

Over her head, Cade motioned away the officers who would have interrupted them. There was plenty of time for questioning. Later. Right now, Laurel needed time to soak in all that had happened. She needed her own time to heal.

"He was such a nice guy, Cade," she said, her mind still incapable of seeing Boomer as a murderer. "Everyone liked him. Who knew that behind that smile was a bitter, resentful heart? That he blamed other people for things only *he* viewed as shortcomings? No one else thought less of him because he didn't have a degree."

"He didn't like himself," Cade murmured in agreement. He continued to stroke her hair, whispering sweet words of nothing while she cried quietly into his shirt, dampening the front of it.

"I'm such a mess," she finally said, pulling back and wiping her eyes.

His smile was indulgent. "I think you've earned the right."

"I guess the police want to question me now." She wrinkled her nose at the thought.

"Yes, but I'm sure the worst of it can wait."

"Oh! My parents!" Laurel realized, putting her hand over her mouth. "They're waiting dinner on me!"

"Why don't you call them and say you'll just be a few minutes late?" Cade suggested. "I'll speak with Chel and the other officers to ask them to keep it short. You can go down to the station tomorrow and give your full statement."

"Right." She patted her pockets, surprised not to find her cell phone. "My phone's in the car," she remembered. "I was on my way over there when all this began."

"You speak with Chel, and I'll get your phone." He pressed a kiss onto her forehead before releasing her.

"Cade?" she called after him as he reached the door.

"Yeah?"

"Can I tell my mom to set the table for one more?"

That slow, sexy smile of his lit the detective's handsome face, helping to chase away some of the shadows in Laurel's heart.

Both of them were oblivious to the others in the crowded living room.

"I'd like that," Cade answered quietly, holding her eyes.

Tonight brought an end to many things. The mystery around Professor Tonchev's death. The break-ins at her beloved Craftsman. To Laurel's brief-lived suspension at the hospital, and to Boomer's career there. With luck, tonight would bring an end to the hostility between her and Nurse Winslow, or would at least help them forge a truce. And tonight undoubtedly brought an end to her friendship with the once-lovable technician everyone called Boomer.

But tonight also ushered in a new beginning. A beginning to her peace of mind. A beginning to sleeping the whole night through, no longer frightened of an intruder. A beginning of healing for the professor's family, and for the injured Dawn Dyson.

Best of all, tonight brought a new beginning for her and Cade.

And, suddenly, Laurel couldn't wait to see what the future held.

Thank you so much for reading my story! Please continue to follow Laurel, Cade, the Curly Girls, and the rest of the hard-working crew at *Texas General* in the rest of the series and in its companion series, Texas General Cozy Cases of Romance.

Still can't get enough? You can catch a glimpse of your favorite medical team and cowboy detective in select *The Sisters, Texas Mystery Series* books, such as *Rose by Any Other Name*, *Bye, Buy Baby* and *Murder Worth a Thousand Words*.

Finally, if you've enjoyed this book, please take a moment to share your thoughts about it with other readers. **It's the single best way to thank an author**, and to ensure more books will follow.

After leaving your review on Amazon, BookBub, Goodreads, and/or the venue of your choice, please drop in for an e-visit at beckiwillis.ccp@gmail.com. I'd love to hear from you!

You can also keep tabs on my latest books by visiting my website, signing up for my not-so-monthly newsletter, or visiting my somewhat neglected social media accounts.

Again, thanks for reading!

ABOUT THE AUTHOR

Best-selling indie author Becki Willis loves crafting stories with believable characters in believable situations. Many of her stories stem from her own travels and from personal experiences. (No worries; she's never actually murdered anyone).

When she's not plotting danger and adventure for her imaginary friends, Becki enjoys reading, antiquing (aka junking), unraveling a good mystery (real or imagined), dark chocolate, and a good cup of coffee. A professed history geek, Becki often weaves pieces of the past into her novels. Family is a central theme in her stories and in her life. She and her husband enjoy traveling, but believe coming home to their Texas ranch is the best part of any trip.

Becki has won numerous awards, but the real compliments come from her readers. Drop in for an e-visit anytime at beckiwillis.ccp@gmail.com, or www.beckiwillis.com.

Made in United States
North Haven, CT
16 June 2022

20311947R00114